D1509535

ASK THE STREETS FOR MERCY   1

THE

ASK STREETS FOR

MERCY

NATIONAL BESTSELLING AUTHOR

T. STYLES

By T. STYLES

Are You On Our Email List?

Sign up on our website

WWW.THECARTELPUBLICATIONS.COM

Or text the word: CARTELBOOKS to 22828

For Prizes, Contests, etc.

CHECK OUT OTHER TITLES BY

THE CARTEL PUBLICATIONS

SHYT LIST 1: BE CAREFUL WHO YOU CROSS
SHYT LIST 2: LOOSE CANNON
SHYT LIST 3: AND A CHILD SHALL LEAVE THEM
SHYT LIST 4: CHILDREN OF THE WRONGED
SHYT LIST 5: SMOKIN' CRAZIES THE FINALE'
PITBULLS IN A SKIRT 1
PITBULLS IN A SKIRT 2
PITBULLS IN A SKIRT 3: THE RISE OF LIL C
PITBULLS IN A SKIRT 4: KILLER KLAN
PITBULLS IN A SKIRT 5: THE FALL FROM GRACE
POISON 1
POISON 2
VICTORIA'S SECRET
HELL RAZOR HONEYS 1
HELL RAZOR HONEYS 2
BLACK AND UGLY
BLACK AND UGLY AS EVER
MISS WAYNE & THE QUEENS OF DC
BLACK AND THE UGLIEST
A HUSTLER'S SON
A HUSTLER'S SON 2
THE FACE THAT LAUNCHED A THOUSAND BULLETS
YEAR OF THE CRACKMOM
THE UNUSUAL SUSPECTS
LA FAMILIA DIVIDED
RAUNCHY
RAUNCHY 2: MAD'S LOVE
RAUNCHY 3: JAYDEN'S PASSION
MAD MAXXX: CHILDREN OF THE CATACOMBS (EXTRA RAUNCHY)
KALI: RAUNCHY RELIVED: THE MILLER FAMILY
REVERSED
QUITA'S DAYSCARE CENTER
QUITA'S DAYSCARE CENTER 2
DEAD HEADS
DRUNK & HOT GIRLS
PRETTY KINGS
PRETTY KINGS 2: SCARLETT'S FEVER
PRETTY KINGS 3: DENIM'S BLUES
PRETTY KINGS 4: RACE'S RAGE
HERSBAND MATERIAL
UPSCALE KITTENS
WAKE & BAKE BOYS
YOUNG & DUMB
YOUNG & DUMB: VYCE'S GETBACK
TRANNY 911
TRANNY 911: DIXIE'S RISE
FIRST COMES LOVE, THEN COMES MURDER
LUXURY TAX
THE LYING KING
CRAZY KIND OF LOVE

BY T. STYLES

WWW.THECARTELPUBLICATIONS.COM

ASK THE STREETS FOR MERCY

By

T. STYLES

Copyright © 2020 by The Cartel Publications.
All rights reserved.
No part of this book may be reproduced in any
form without permission
from the author, except by reviewer who may
quote passages
to be printed in a newspaper or magazine.

PUBLISHER'S NOTE:
This book is a work of fiction. Names,
characters, businesses,
Organizations, places, events and incidents
are the product of the
Author's imagination or are used fictionally.
Any resemblance of
Actual persons, living or dead, events, or
locales are entirely coincidental.

ISBN 10: 1948373289
ISBN 13: 978-1948373289

Cover Design: Davida Baldwin
www.oddballdsgn.com

First Edition
Printed in the United States of America

What Up Fam,

I hope you all are staying safe! I'm going to make this short and sweet...ASK THE STREETS FOR MERCY is a crazzzzzy roller coaster ride! Make sure you don't blink because you may miss something! (Insert Dr. Evil laugh).

Don't forget, if you're not registered to vote, please go to: https://www.voteamerica.com/register-to-vote/ today and show up on Tuesday, November 3, 2020. It's imperative!

With that being said, keeping in line with tradition, we want to give respect to a vet or new trailblazer paving the way. In this novel, we would like to recognize:

RuPaul Charles

RuPaul Andre Charles is an American Drag Queen, author, actor, model, singer...and the list goes on and on. I always knew RuPaul was a star, but I just recently started binging *RuPaul's Drag Race* and I fell in love with him. TV show aside, he's all about building people up and love. And in this world today, love is extremely important so thank you RuPaul!

Aight Fam, I'ma leave ya'll to it! We'll talk to you again soon!

God Bless!

Charisse "C. Wash" Washington
Vice President
The Cartel Publications
www.thecartelpublications.com
www.facebook.com/publishercwash
Instagram: publishercwash
www.twitter.com/cartelbooks
www.facebook.com/cartelpublications
Follow us on Instagram: Cartelpublications
#CartelPublications
#UrbanFiction
#PrayForCece
#RuPaul

#ASKTHESTREETSFORMERCY

BY T. STYLES

We see only what we want to see.

We remember only what justifies our pain.

And if we aren't careful, a shift occurs.

This is the beginning of madness.

CHAPTER 1

THE PAST

1988

I t was eventide.

As she ran.

Fast.

While she made her escape, tiny shards of many disposed liquor bottles stabbed through the heel of her foot. Due to the frail ghost like figures who hung within the darkness of these spaces to pump poison through their veins, she also felt the tip of a needle piercing into the sole of the other.

She wasn't concerned.

The only thing on fifteen-year-old Darcy Dupree's mind was her eight-year-old little brother Levyne, who's hand was clasped firmly into her own. And Rasha, her twelve-month-old baby sister, who she gripped so tightly against her budding breasts, the child could barely breathe.

"I'll keep you safe," Darcy chanted to them both. Her gaze fell on her baby sister. She smelled of spoiled milk and the feces that soiled her pamper. "As long as

I'm alive, I will always watch over you. Unlike me, you will have peace."

It was a promise she made from the moment she saw the amniotic fluid covering Rasha's face. Her mother had given birth early, after being beaten by a group of women at a party, who felt her lighter skin afforded her some unknown privilege.

Barely alive, and clutching her belly, when she traipsed to her apartment building, it was her thirteen-year-old daughter who greeted her in the hallway where she collapsed on the stairwell.

Sensing its mother's fear, the infant pushed and prodded within the womb to be free. Within minutes, Rasha Dupree was born in fear and bathed in blood. To make matters more insane, Darcy watched her mother take her last breath, and her sister take her first into a hateful world.

Rasha's father, Lester, who returned home later that night, after being with another woman, walked over her body and toward the door as paramedics worked desperately to save her life.

"Don't look at me like that, girl." He said to Darcy. "I'm all you got now. And you'll need me, long before I need you."

She prayed he wasn't right.

When he demonstrated such a callous act using his words, there was a smile on his face that Darcy never forgot. Almost as if he were relieved that her mother was gone.

And Darcy believed she knew why.

He was the living embodiment to the boogeyman. He was the monster who crept into children's rooms at night, destroying their childhoods in the process. And so, as Darcy held her baby sister in her arm, she vowed to protect her always.

And that is exactly what she was trying to do.

After running so far that trash along the baselines of rowhomes transposed into flowerpots and small gardens, indicating she was now in a wealthy neighborhood, she paused when she happened upon an opened garage connected to a brownstone. Looking behind herself for the assailant, she dipped inside.

Standing next to a late model white Benz, when her butt brushed against it, she could feel its warmth. She was certain someone just returned home, probably from the grocers, and failed to close the door.

To her it was a sign from God.

After all, she prayed hard.

"Where we going?" Levyne asked as he was pulled inside. His eyes were as wide as his face, and his eyelashes were as fluffy as dandelions.

"Shhhh." She placed a longer finger against her lips.

"But I want to —."

Still gripping Rasha, Darcy bent down to stare him in the eyes. "Listen, we goin' some place safe. Now I don't know where yet, but we going together. Okay? But you gotta be quiet."

His sister didn't often use thunder when talking to him. But this was no play time and he had better be quiet.

"Okay." He nodded.

She stood up, looked to her right. There was a door and she opened it, welcoming herself into someone's house. It was a bold move, but when it came to her siblings, she would kill to see them safe.

Once inside, the first thing that hit her was the sweet smell of potpourri. It was such a stark difference from the odors of sex, fried chicken, curry and death that left its footing in the apartment building she lived in Baltimore City with her father.

She reasoned that money had a way of cleaning the air.

It was somewhat true.

Slowly she ascended the steps leading further into the house despite not knowing where she was going. When she looked down, she saw thousands of ants, which she and her friends referred to as 'white people roaches' marching in armies along the staircase and she wondered why they were so deep.

"Who are you?" Joe Hern asked walking into the house. He was a tall white man in his late forties with piercing blue eyes. There was both a kindness and danger in his expression.

Which personality would he offer her this night?

"I said, who are you?" He tossed his keys on the table next to the couch. They slammed against it before sliding to the floor.

"I'm...I..." Darcy's voice was trapped in her throat.

"Joe, what's going on?" Nancy Hern asked entering the living room from upstairs. She was a short stalky white woman with light red hair, that clearly wanted to clock out for life, allowing the greying roots to do its job. "Who are these people?" She pulled the strings of her robe tighter, squeezing her body in half.

"I don't know." He said before walking up to Darcy. "She hasn't told me yet. Although I'm still waiting."

Darcy opened her mouth to talk but still no words exited. Why couldn't she speak? Surely, she saw this coming when she decided to break and enter. "I...I'm..."

"This my sister." Levyne said raising his chin.

Joe smiled at the boy. "Okay." He nodded. "So, what are you doing in my house?"

He shrugged. "I don't know." He looked up at her. "What we doing in these white peoples—."

She yanked him quiet and took a deep breath. "My sister, and I...all of us...we in trouble."

He frowned. "Trouble how?"

"I'm going to lock the door in case more of 'em try to get inside." Nancy said running down the steps leading to the garage.

"Can I, can we sit down?" Darcy asked looking at the white luxurious couch to her left.

He nodded.

She sat on the sofa and tugged at her brother who stared at the man in awe. He wasn't used to seeing vanilla colored faces. Darcy on the other hand tried to tuck her bloody feet under the couch, to prevent angering the hosts.

"Sit down, L."

He flopped next to her.

"I need somewhere safe, sir. I ain't, I ain't got no money but—."

"Have you considered calling the police?" Nancy asked returning to the room. "Because this makes me uncomfortable. We aren't harboring criminals. Why, this is our home." She placed a liver spotted hand over her heart. "And we are law abiding citizens who just returned home from the grocery store and—"

"I understand, ma'am. And I ain't, I mean, I wouldn't be here if I had a choice." Tears streamed down Darcy's face and she gripped Rasha tighter. "I try and be strong. My brother, he's, he's not at risk but my baby sister is. And I don't want him opening up her body like he, like he—."

"Opening up your body?" Nancy yelled. She knew the girl was nasty. "What are you, some sort of prostitute or something?"

Darcy glared at the insult. "No ma'am. I ain't ever give my body away for money a day in my life."

Upon hearing her shivering voice, Joe's heart softened but he could feel the stinging eyeball rays of his wife upon him. "We need more information if you want my assistance."

"Sir, all I can say right now is I'm askin' for help. The kinda help that people like you ain't gotta give me." She pleaded with her eyes. "And I know we come from different backgrounds and all. And different worlds too." She looked around from where she sat. "I mean, I ain't ever sat on a sofa this nice in my life."

I bet you haven't. Nancy frowned. Having a nice sofa was one of the reasons she wanted them out in the first place.

"Like I'm tryin' to say, I don't wanna mess up what you got here, sir. Just need a little help is all. Please."

"What does help look like for you?"

"Sir, I'ma need to stay here for the night. And maybe make a few calls in the morning."

Silence filled the room.

Even the ants appeared to go on pause.

After all, what Darcy was asking was major. Essentially, she was begging to stay in his home even if for a short time. And since she didn't know him, she was almost certain he would deny her request.

But fortune favors the bold.

And doing nothing devours the helpless.

"I'm hungry," Levyne said out of left field.

Really, he wasn't. But the home was the richest place he'd ever been so he figured the food would taste like gold. But they weren't there for that, and so Darcy pinched him on the thigh.

"Ouch!"

"Then stop begging."

"But you're begging too."

She smiled reached into her pocket and stuffed something into his mouth. Both Joe and Nancy looked at one another but kept their opinions to themselves.

What did she give the boy?

"I'll feed you later. Right now, we—."

"Make them something to eat, honey," Joe ordered Nancy.

"Wait, are you, are you sure?" Darcy asked. "Because I don't, I don't want to put you out."

"Yes, I'm sure." Joe nodded.

"Honey, I don't have food in the house for children." Nancy said with a hanging jaw. "What we bought tonight is for the dinner party tomorrow. And with my diet I—."

"But you said you just went to the grocery store." Levyne said.

Darcy pinched him again and whispered into his ear. His body stiffened and it was almost as if he turned into a mannequin.

Joe cleared his throat. "Um, Nancy, just make the children something to eat. I'll go to the store tomorrow and buy plenty of food for you and loud-mouthed Freda to stuff your faces with."

She glared at Darcy and then focused on Joe. "Sure, honey, anything you say." She stomped away.

When she was gone, he said, "Listen, this isn't normally something I'd do. Allowing strangers into my home in this day and age is dangerous." He started. "So, before you ask for more than a meal, the answer will be no."

She nodded. "Okay. I...I understand."

"Welp, I guess we're going to die," Levyne whispered, his eyes closing slightly.

Upon hearing his words, Joe took a deep breath. "You can stay one night."

"Joe!" Nancy yelled from the kitchen slamming a pot on top of the stove.

"Are you cooking or talking?"

She rolled her eyes and continued about the kitchen in amazing rage. The cabinets were getting the business that's for sure.

"I really appreciate this," Darcy whispered placing a hand over her heart. "I don't know what I expected but...but this wasn't it."

CABINET SLAM!

Joe sat next to her. "We have the space." CABINET SLAM! "Most of the rooms I haven't seen in months to be honest. We bought the house because we wanted more footage and don't even use it all."

There it was...

The extreme kindness she heard about from strangers but never thought existed. "I will never forget your—"

"But I'm not done." He raised his hand.

CABINET SLAM!

"If you stay here." He continued. "That is, if I allow you this favor, I need more than what you've told me already. So, if I'm going to trust you, you have to trust me. It's the only way."

She nodded and Levyne's heavy head fell on her arm. "I understand."

"So, what's going on?" He continued.

She cleared her throat. "My father he...he does..." Suddenly she broke down, as her brother stroked her arm with gritty, dirty fingertips.

"Don't worry about it," Joe said realizing they were going to a dark place. "Just wash up so that you can eat. I think I have some milk for the little one too. And maybe we can make a homemade pamper. She smells like she needs a changing." He pinched Rasha's cheek. "When you're done, I'll show you your beds."

She sniffled and wiped her tears away. "Thank you, sir. Thank…thank you."

The next morning, when the alarm went off Joe shoved the comforters back and slammed his palm on the clock to stop the noise. When he turned around, his wife was sitting on the side of the bed with her back in his direction. He could tell by how stiff her shoulders were, that she had not only been up for hours, but that she rehearsed her anger all night.

Basically, in addition to the sunshine, trouble was ready to greet his ass.

Lying face up, he wiped the crust from his eyes and sighed. "I couldn't turn them away, honey."

"You could have. You just chose not to." She shrugged, back still in his direction. "And you put our marriage on the line for those…those…"

"Don't say it." He rolled his head to look at her. "You're a better woman than that, Nancy. Don't make me look at you differently."

"Those people!" She jumped up and stood at the foot of the bed. "What is it with you?" She threw her arms up in the air. "Why do you feel the need to...to always help? If they don't care about themselves, why should you?"

"Maybe you should eat sugar again. Your attitude has been—."

"Fuck you, Joe!"

He glared. "Easy, Nancy. I'm losing seconds with you."

"I don't mean to be disrespectful, but I haven't touched sugar in years. She continued. "You know that!"

"Well, maybe you should. Your mood has been horrible."

"Why are you doing this?" She threw her hands up. "Huh, tell me!"

"Because we have to start helping, Nancy."

"Who?"

"Us."

She frowned. "Do you mean...white people...oh, Joe, please."

"It goes deeper." He took a deep breath. "When this country was built, black people—."

"Joe, I don't want to hear it!" She waved a thick hand across the room.

"Listen to me!" He yelled.

She sighed and shook her head.

"When this country was built, it was run by the white man and black woman." His voice was calm but serious.

She turned a deep shade of red. "How you figure?"

"White men made laws and gave orders to the slaves that they were expected to follow through. But it was the black woman, who ran the house, raised our children and their own, which as we know became slaves. And if we want to heal, the white man and black woman will have to lead the world to a balance." He sighed. "And so, when I saw Darcy, I figured what better place to start than now."

"Joe, you sound crazy."

"You can think what you want."

"The way I feel now, I could care less about helping anybody." She was so angry she trembled. "And never tell that story again." She pointed at him. "Never tell anyone."

He smiled, shook his head and grabbed his eyeglasses off the side of the bed. "Nancy, you know

better than to warn me. We both know who runs this—
."

A BABY CRIED IN THE DISTANCE.

Joe looked at the door and sat on the edge of the bed. His feet nestled into the thick white carpeting.

"That child has been crying on and off all morning." She said. "It's very annoying."

"What you mean all morning?" He stood up. "The girl didn't see to her? She seemed so protective over—"

"Like I said, they don't care about their people, why should we?"

Slowly, Joe walked out and toward the room he assigned to Darcy and her siblings for the night. From the outside of the door, he could hear the baby crying louder.

He softly knocked on his own property.

No answer.

Looking back at Nancy, he faced the door again and opened it carefully. The baby was on the bed alone. The moment she saw his face, she stopped crying and began to laugh playfully. And then for reasons unknown, she cried again. As if she were trying on her voice to see which one fit.

Would she bring rage or peace into the world?

In the moment she didn't seem sure.

BY T. STYLES

Connected to her pink onesie was a letter held firmly with a large safety pin.

"What is that?" She asked covering her heart.

"I don't know." They walked toward the child and he unpinned the letter.

It simply read:

I'm sorry.

The baby yelled louder.

"This is madness! She's making too much noise." Nancy said as she went to lift the infant who cried louder. But the baby couldn't be bothered and wanted her hands up off her. "What is wrong with her?"

"Put her down, Nancy."

"No, I have her."

"Put her down!"

She tossed the baby and she bounced once on the mattress and hiccupped. She was silent for a brief moment due to deliria only to cry again seconds later.

Joe, confused at why Darcy left, continued to read the sentence as if another clue was hidden on the ripped-up page. When he realized it wasn't, he dropped the letter on the floor and flopped on the bed. Looking up at his wife, he sighed deeply just as Rasha crawled into his arms.

Just that easily the baby appeared to be in heaven.

The baby was at peace.

And Nancy was livid.

She turned for the door.

"Where are you going?"

Silence.

"Make her some warm milk while you at it!" He advised.

Slowly she exited and tromped toward the living room. When she saw Darcy's bloody footprints on her hardwood floors, and on the bottom of the couch, she was angry times two. Stomping into the kitchen she grabbed the sugar jar and a large spoon which was as big as a ladle.

Removing the lid, she walked through the living room, while shoving spoonful's into her mouth as she sobbed.

On the way to the garage door, sugar granules that missed her gullet, fell onto the floor and upon the army of ants, which were waiting patiently to get snacked up.

After all, this happened every day.

Because Nancy was a woman who was never at peace.

Nancy was a woman unworthy of raising sane kids.

And this made her dangerous.

BY T. STYLES

CHAPTER 2

FIVE YEARS LATER

1993

Christmas was in the air…

As Joe and Nancy Hern went about preparing for their yearly holiday party, six-year-old Rasha sat on a chair at the island in the kitchen, with a smile. Holding a gingerbread cookie too big for her face, she loved the energy this night brought. Besides, when the guests rolled in, there was bound to be one person or another begging to see the pretty black girl with the almond colored skin and wispy curls surrounding her face.

And she loved attention.

The more the better.

The child was stunning. But what made her unique, were her legs, which were far more muscular than girls her age, and Joe didn't know why.

But there was a hidden reason.

There's always a reason.

Anyway, during the times when their friends would come over, Nancy would be forced to recant how Joe came about caring for the child that *'nobody wanted'*. To his friends he was a hero. A blue-eyed Jesus who rescued a child from the depths of hell.

But to Rasha, he was simply daddy.

And to Joe, she was simply his little girl.

Looking over at her husband as he fussed with the eggnog, she shook her head. "I don't know why you like that drink. It's so sweet. I keep telling you sugar will kill you. That's why I haven't touched the stuff in over six years."

Again, she touched it every day.

And had every pound, including twenty more, to show for it.

"Not everyone is on a diet," He slapped her butt and then pinched Rasha's cute nose. It was almost as if, if he gave one of them attention, he had to give the other attention too. "Not even your chubby friend Freda."

"My best friend isn't fat. Leave her alone."

He chuckled. "I'm just joking. Still, let me and Rasha have our fun."

She shook her head. "Aw, hush and grab the macaroni and cheese out of the oven. And then put it on the counter."

"Did you remind Aaron and his wife not to bring any meals?" He asked. "Last time he brought a peanut casserole and just smelling it gave me a reaction."

"Stop whining," she said playfully.

"It's not funny!" He said growing serious. "I could've died."

Rasha giggled at his rage and Nancy looked at her with a side eye.

The child silenced instantly.

"Joe, of course I told him." She cleared her throat and walked out of the kitchen with a tower of drinking glasses in her hand to position them around the dining room table.

Joe placed the ladle he was stirring the drink with, next to Rasha. The eggnog along with the sweet odor of the cake, was intoxicating. And she licked her lips in anticipation of its flavor.

Reaching to take a lick her surrogate said, "Oh no you don't." He squeezed her nose slightly again. "You already talked me into giving you that cookie before dinner. You won't catch me giving you a taste of liquor too."

"That's because we don't need her gaining weight." She walked into the kitchen, touched the little girl softly on the back and winked.

Rasha jumped at her touch.

"But I know she's your favorite so I can't much blame you for spoiling her rotten." Nancy continued. "Did you grab the macaroni and cheese like I asked?"

He looked at Rasha and made a face. "Nope, too busy talking to my *favorite* girl. I was getting to it though." He moved out of her way as she yanked open the oven's door with an attitude.

Removing the macaroni and cheese she smiled at the succulent dish. "This is beautiful."

Joe stood next to her and eyed the meal in awe. "Laurie sure does no how to make 'em doesn't she?"

She frowned. "I helped her you know?"

"Sure you did." He slapped her butt.

"As much as you hit me on my ass it should be blue by now."

"You can handle it." He looked down at his watch. "Oh no, almost forgot the drinks. Let me go grab the wine before the store closes." He snatched his keys off the wall and kissed Rasha. "Be back."

Rasha grabbed his hand. "Can I go?"

Nancy looked at her and focused on the dish she was washing in the sink. "You need to stop begging, Rasha. Don't worry, the man's coming back."

He looked down at her. "I won't leave you. Trust me."

BY T. STYLES

Slowly she released his hand. But she was always worried about being abandoned. Always worried about being unloved. And it shaped her personality every day.

"Okay, honey." Nancy's back was still turned as she busied herself with the sink. "See you when you get back."

But the moment the door closed, Rasha sat the cookie down on the counter and looked at Nancy.

The mood grew intense.

Slowly Nancy turned around. Her eyes were dark and evil as she focused on the child with unwanted attention. "How many days?"

Rasha swallowed and in a low voice said, "Two thousand and twenty-eight days and —."

"LOUDER, GIRL!"

Rasha trembled and her curls shook. "Two thousand and twenty-eight days!"

"No." She grinned sinisterly. "It's been two thousand and thirty days since your sister left you. Do you know why?"

"Yes."

"Let me hear the words."

"Because nobody loves me."

She laughed. "That's right, because even when she was here, she couldn't stand to look at you." She opened the drawer and grabbed a spoon. "Because whenever she looked at you..." she yanked the sugar jar and shoveled a heap into her mouth. "She was reminded at how much she hated you. And you will never see her again. Because she abandoned you. And everyone you ever meet will do the same. Everyone you meet will make fun of you. Now say it."

"I will never see her again."

"Again!" Sugar fell to the floor as ants began the busy work of picking up the pieces.

"*I will never see her again.*" She chanted so long, she put herself into a trance-like state. "*I will never see her again. I will never see her again. I will —.*"

She raised her hand, silencing her instantly. "Now, did you clean your room?" She put the sugar and spoon back in its place.

Wiping the tears away that crept up she said, "Yes, ma'am."

"Why don't I believe that?" She walked to the refrigerator and removed a bowl of potato salad. "Because you and I both know, you're horrible at keeping up your room. Since you have a tendency to want to be up under Joe so much."

"I did clean my room, ma'am. I promise."

She grabbed a big wooden spoon and stirred the salad with unnecessary force. Almost turning it into nasty mashed potatoes. And as she continued to whip, Rasha had a moment. Today she would speak up for herself.

"Daddy won't abandon me."

This was her first act of rebellion.

But it wouldn't be her last.

"He isn't your fucking daddy!" She yelled, slamming a flat palm on the counter. "He isn't any relation to you." She released the wooden spoon into the bowl. "All you are is a burden. And I'll be glad when you do us a service and leave."

Rasha's bottom lip trembled, but she held back the tears.

Eying the gingerbread she sat on the counter Nancy said, "Eat the cookie."

Rasha shook her head no.

Slowly, Nancy walked to the side of the counter. Looking down at her she said, "Eat the fucking cookie."

"I don't want—"

Nancy slapped her as tears rolled down her own face. Her soul was in turmoil for how she was treating the child, but she couldn't stop. Why did she hate her so? "I said eat the fucking cookie! Now!"

Slowly Rasha picked up the cookie which collapsed under the pressure, dropping crumbs everywhere. As she chewed, and Nancy watched her devour every bite, she went about sweeping.

Wiping her hands on her apron Nancy said, "Now that you've eaten my food, you know what you have to do right?"

Rasha nodded yes.

"In life, all debts must be paid." She pointed to the stairs that led upwards.

A few seconds later they were in the small gym within the house. The room was built for Nancy, but she hadn't used the treadmill since it was installed. Stating that she'd been losing so much weight, it was no longer necessary.

But she never used it once.

However, Rasha had.

Many, many, many times.

As directed, Rasha ran on the treadmill while Nancy sat on a recliner drinking eggnog. After a minute, Rasha looked back at her. "I'm sleepy. May I go to bed?"

"I thought you wanted to go to our party. So, everyone could see your pretty-fucking-little-face."

"I'm tired."

"No, you aren't...run."

Having done so many times before, Rasha increased the speed and ran faster. And after what seemed like forever, the lunch Joe shared with her earlier in the day, in conjunction with the cookie, rolled around in her belly causing her to feel queasy.

"Faster."

Rasha ran quicker.

"Faster!"

Rasha increased the speed.

"Faster!"

Rasha ran so fast, her body toppled off the treadmill as she slammed against the floor. But there was no sympathy in Nancy's eyes or heart. And so, after drinking her eggnog, and licking the glass, she rose and stood over the child's exhausted body. "Now you're tired. Feel the difference?"

"Why don't you like me?" Rasha said, as her chest rose up and down.

"Because you chose not to love me."

The Christmas dinner party was a major success...

Six of the Hern's friends were seated around the dining room table, laughing, drinking and talking about life. Always on duty, their thirty-eight-year-old maid Laurie tended to all of their needs as they got drunker by the glass.

Laurie had worked for the Hern's forever and knew when to step off and when to return. So, they frequently forgot she was even around. A skilled caregiver, she was often forced to attend to their every need, even if their needs were not articulated. But beneath the tough exterior was a woman who was tired. Was a woman who was in emotional pain.

But now it was breaktime.

And so, when every glass was filled and every plate was packed, she trekked upstairs toward Rasha's room. The little girl had become her favorite part about caring for the family. To say she loved her was an understatement.

When she opened the bedroom door, and saw Rasha lying on her side, hugging a doll almost her size, her heart dropped. There was a language that only the two shared, that didn't need words. The moment Rasha saw her face, she released the doll from incarceration, hopped out of bed and rushed toward her. Wrapping her arms around her legs, she hugged her tightly.

Laurie smiled widely as she hoisted her up and walked her over to her bed. Placing her down, she sat next to her on the small mattress. Next she picked up the doll and smiled at it while examining its features. It was brown, with long black hair and pink rosy cheeks.

"I had a doll somewhat like this." She sighed. "That's why I gave it to you." Her accent was light and soft as a rose petal. "When I was lonely, in Mexico, my father would buy me one on my worst days. I had many lonely days, bebe. So, in the end I had many dolls too."

Rasha looked at the toy. "I love her."

"Dolls are not much different than people you know?" She looked at her. "And if you ask me, they're better."

"Why?"

"Because you can talk to them. And they will listen, without hurting your feelings. Without abandoning you."

Rasha looked down at the doll. In her mind she was right. She always had the fear of being left or abandoned, even by Joe, but the doll was always in her life. The doll was always there.

Laurie pinched her nose. "So, how are you?"

"Tired."

"Did you eat?"

She shook her head no.

"Why not, Rasha? I told you, you have to eat to be healthy and strong. I don't want you withering down to bones." She tickled her lightly and she laughed for the first time since Nancy terrorized her on the treadmill.

"If I eat, I have to pay for my food."

"Pay for your food?" She laughed. "No, you don't. You're just a little girl."

Rasha nodded because she thought so too, but that wasn't her life. And so, slowly she began to cry. "I don't...I don't like it here sometimes."

"Why? Joe loves you."

"I love him too."

"Then what is it, bebe?"

"Nancy. She's...she's mean to me when daddy isn't around. And I—."

"What are you doing in here?" Nancy asked opening the door.

Laurie popped up and put her arms behind her back. "I...I was just checking on Rasha."

Rasha crawled in bed and hid under the sheets.

"Unless you want to be at your own fucking house since you'll be fired, I suggest you get back downstairs." When she left Nancy walked up to the bed. "I know what you're doing. And it won't work. Because at the end of the day, this is my house. And it will remain my house long after you're gone."

It was summer and Rasha and Joe were coming back from a carnival. Since Nancy wasn't one for rides or sugary snacks, in public anyway, Rasha was happy she could spend the time alone with Joe. When she started noticing familiar landmarks leading back to their brownstone, her stomach churned.

She didn't want to go home.

Since she was in a good mood all day, he noticed. "Rasha...are you okay?"

Scared to tell him the truth, she thought of a lie instead. After all, would he be receptive to knowing that the woman he made his wife was a monster?

"Yes. I'm...I'm fine."

He smiled and continued to drive. "Did I ever tell you how you came to be with me?"

She shook her head no.

"Your sister brought you and your brother to the house. She was concerned that you would be hurt, and she wanted you to be safe."

"I have a brother?"

"Of course you do. Your sister was doing all she could that night to keep you both safe."

Hearing mention of her sister in a good way made her hot with rage. Literally and physically hot. In her humble opinion if Darcy cared so much, why would she leave her to rot like Nancy said? Why didn't she come back to make sure she was okay?

Why! Why! Why!

"If it's true, why did she leave me?"

"She was young, Rasha. Young and brave. And you should be proud. So very proud."

"That doesn't answer the question, Poppy."

He nodded because it was true. "She felt like we were in a better position to take care of you financially."

She looked down at her fingertips. There was a hangnail on one, and she focused on it with all her might. "That's not what Nancy says."

Joe frowned. "What did she say?"

Silence. He wasn't ready for the rip down, she was certain.

"Listen, Nancy is sad, Rasha. In fact, she believes she's doing a good job with you. But she's a very sad woman and sometimes sad people can project what they feel onto others. Never be that way. Always remember the good things."

She looked up at him. "Why is she sad?"

"When she was a little girl, and her mother died from a trip and fall accident, her older sister took care of her for a little while. And then, when the sister met someone, well, she felt she didn't have time to care for her anymore. I don't know why she is giving you these vibes. But I believe it's unconsciously to see how another person handles the same problem she dealt with. And it's your job to show her your strength. If you want, I can talk to her for you so — ."

"No!"

He nodded. "Okay. But trust me, she cares about you."

Rasha heard him but she couldn't get past the hate in Nancy's eyes. "She says you aren't my real father."

He looked out the window and frowned, before turning back to Rasha. "I consider myself to be your father." He paused. "I also happen to believe that being a father isn't always about blood. Being a father means taking care of someone. Of raising a person. And of loving a person. And although I never knew how special you would be to me, I understand now. So, I consider you my daughter. That is, if you don't mind."

She looked down.

He raised her chin. "I'll never leave you. Even if I'm gone, I'll still be with you."

If he loved her so much, she decided to kick the truth to see how it landed. "I don't like Nancy."

"Listen, Rasha, it's important for me that you get along with my wife." The way he said *wife* cut different. Like a smile from a stranger, followed by a frown when they thought you turned your head. "I'll be called out of town for three months. So, it'll be just you and her. You have to get along. And…"

She could still hear his voice but suddenly her head got heavy. Unable to control its own weight, her face crashed against the window.

After Rasha passed out in his car, Joe was grief stricken. It took friends who were doctors to tell him that she was probably just sad about him leaving and

BY T. STYLES

that it was safe to go out of town for his business trip. In their opinion, caring for a child was mostly woman's work anyway, and so Nancy would be fine. They even agreed to help her with anything she needed.

"Don't worry, Joe." Nancy said one night as they were getting ready for bed. We'll be okay. Trust me."

"She seems to think you don't like her, Nancy." He said as he packed his bag.

"I know, which is why I will make her health and happiness my top priority. You can trust me." She presented a huge smile. To outsiders it was fake as fuck, but he didn't get the message. He needed them to get along. After all, what was he going to do? Lug a child around? "It's gonna be just us girls."

And so, he left for work to Arizona for a three-month project, leaving them alone. But things went downhill when the following week, Nancy fired Laurie, the only person on earth Rasha felt was in her corner. A month later, the visits from Joe's friends stopped, and Joe was so busy he barely had time to phone home on most days. And as a result, Nancy no longer had eyes upon her as she terrorized Rasha in secret, coming up with new ways to alter her young mind.

Still, Rasha took it all.

And appeared to have gotten stronger.

But the hate Nancy felt toward the child grew heavier after one night when Nancy had her friend Freda over. The two were sitting in the dining room, at the table, drinking red wine by the bottle. And since Joe was not there to stop his wife from being nasty, she and her friend took to demeaning the child as they made her stand in front of them as if she were on display.

"You should be grateful," Freda said with a southern accent so thick, every word out of her mouth sounded like she was singing. Every time she spoke, she would comb her fingers through her bleach blonde hair and brittle strands would float to the floor. "Not many black children who are abandoned get an opportunity like this. Show some respect."

Although her opinion was one sided, Nancy grinned, loving that finally someone was on her side. "Do you hear what she's saying. Try a little more gratitude."

Rasha glared. *Fuck these bitches.* She thought.

"Hold up, are you, is she frowning at me, Nancy?" Freda said sitting her glass down on the table.

"No, ma'am." Rasha said shaking her head slowly from left to right.

"Told you she was a nasty bitch." Nancy said, gulping her drink, before pouring another.

Freda yanked Rasha closer, her red chipped nails digging into the flesh of her arm. "Don't you ever look at me like that again? Do you hear me? Ever!"

Horrified and embarrassed, Rasha ran upstairs toward her room. Throwing herself on her bed face first, she cried about how they treated her. She cried about how much she missed Joe and Laurie. And she cried about the blood seeping out of her arm.

While in bed, Rasha remembered all the times Nancy made her chant. She wondered if it would work for other things. And so, she decided to try it.

"I wish she would die. I wish she would die. I wish she would die." Angry at how they made her feel downstairs, Rasha spent the next ten minutes chanting the woman's death repeatedly. Her words of hate continued, even as she heard Nancy saying goodbye downstairs.

As she spoke each word, she gave as much power to them as possible. And for some reason, she began to feel better.

She wanted death for sure.

When she heard the garage door opening, Rasha rushed to the window and chanted harder. She saw Freda pulling out of the garage in her white Honda, and Nancy walking alongside her driver's window while holding a glass of wine.

Still running her mouth of course.

Rasha's chant went from *"I wish she would die,"* to *"DIE, DIE, DIE!"*

The moment the back of the car pulled fully out of the garage, it was rammed into the passenger's side by a navy blue pickup truck that was going too fast.

Shards of glass ripped at Nancy's face from Freda's window, as the car slammed into a lighting poll, and her friend was tossed out of the passenger side window.

Just as Rasha ordered, she was dead on site.

Looking at the catastrophe that she believed she caused, she closed the window and slid down to the floor. Pulling her knees against her chest, she bit down on her tongue. Tasting the salty, metallic flavor of her own blood, she vowed never to speak again.

After losing her best friend, Nancy hated Rasha even more. After all, she only called Freda over to the house because Rasha didn't behave the way she wanted. It was as if she knew about the chanting she was doing upstairs. While the child, filled with guilt, vowed never to talk again, believing her voice was powerful enough to make people die.

Nancy, more than tipsy, one night she entered her room and tossed a pretty red dress in her face. "Get up." Nancy instructed.

Rasha popped out of bed.

"Put on the dress and be downstairs in five minutes."

Rasha nodded as she exited.

Slipping out of her pink flannel pajamas with blue teddy bears throughout, she slid into the dress which was much too mature for her age. It was tight in the wrong places. Shiny. And loud. Still, she wore the garment which once it was on, forced her into womanhood. Making her look too sexual.

Ten minutes later, they were driving down the street in Nancy's white Benz. As she cruised, loud classical music blasted from the speakers. At first, they appeared to be on a joy ride, but within five minutes, they were in a seedy part of Baltimore were crime was rampant.

Driving slowly, she forced her to look at the decrepit homes and buildings as they drove by. "You see, this is where we saved you from. These are your people."

Rasha's heart thumped. Shielded by Joe, she had never been to the hood before and she didn't like what she was seeing.

"Do you want to live here?" Nancy asked.

Rasha shook her head no so hard her neck cracked.

"Why not?"

She swallowed the lump in her throat. She wanted to tell her the reasons why. That she was scared. That she didn't want to be in a strange place alone. But she vowed never to talk and was doing all she could to honor that request.

After all, her words held power.

Feeling in control, Nancy smiled and touched the hem of the dress she was wearing. "Well Joe told me to tell you he's thinking about sending you back. Said he was tired of feeding you. Tired of you living in our home rent free. I tried to tell him no, but he is really thinking long and hard about it."

Rasha trembled.

"Maybe if you're a good little girl than things can change." She shrugged. "Maybe if you love me, life will be better. But I think you need to know how good you have it with us first. I think you need to know what it feels like to be amongst your own." She looked out of the window. "Maybe then you will learn to respect me."

She slowed the car down on a mostly abandoned street in East Baltimore.

Across the way, a crew of hood fellas peered at the car from the steps of an apartment building called The Oxford. It was a brick tenement with a few boarded-up windows scattered throughout. Despite its off-brand look, the inside still held tenants.

Slowly the strangers rose, their hands hovering over their waist as they wondered what the woman was up to. Would they have to protect their land per usual?

"Get out." Nancy said simply.

She shook her head no.

"Get out!" She balled her fists up tightly and banged the steering wheel. "Get out! Get out! Get out!"

Rasha wouldn't leave.

Annoyed, Nancy shoved her car door opened, stormed around the vehicle to the passenger's side. Yanking the door, she dragged Rasha out into the middle of the street by her arms. Her body toppled to the ground and rolled. When she was done, she ran back to her car and pulled off.

From her rearview mirror, she could see Rasha crying in the middle of the road with her pretty red dress. And the men from the steps slowly hovering around her like vultures.

A smile covered her face as she was certain they would do her dirty work.

An hour later, after dumping Rasha off in the streets of Baltimore, Nancy was home preparing which lie to tell Joe. The plan was to call him a bit after midnight, fake like she heard a sound and then go check on her in bed. She figured by that time the streets would have chewed up the pretty young thing and she would be done with her for good.

Standing in front of the mirror, she went to work. "*Oh, Joe, Rasha ran away!*" She practiced. Realizing it wasn't believable enough, she fake cried. "*Oh, Joe, I'm so afraid! I went to check on Rasha around midnight and she's gone! What will we do?*" Loving how she sounded, she decided to go grab a drink until the right time to spit her lies arrived, but her phone rang.

It was Joe.

So, the time was now.

She started not to answer but then decided to talk calmly to him first and then call back later after claiming the child was gone.

"Hello, honey," he said happily. "How are you holding up? With Freda being gone?"

His bright mood made her day. "I'm doing a bit better. It's still hard though. How are you?" She flopped on the sofa, threw her feet up on the glass table and wiggled her toes.

"It's crazy out here but I don't want to complain. There is a lot of interest around the Vupont drug for patients with bipolar disorder but not so much around Vaxent."

"Well at least you and your team were smart enough to bring research on both trials." She grinned and wiped her hair behind her ear.

"You're right about that. If things go well this deal could net the company over a billion." He sighed.

"And a bonus for us too I hope?" She smiled.

"You know it, sweetheart." He chuckled. "So, tell me where you went tonight."

She frowned. "What do you mean?"

"Barbara across the street said she saw you take Rasha out the house earlier. And that you were both wearing dresses. So, where did you go?"

ASK THE STREETS FOR MERCY 53

Nosey bitch. She thought.

She slid her dusty feet off the table and rose. "Oh, I...I mean..." She couldn't get her thoughts together.

"Nancy, where did you go?"

"I didn't take her out." Her face reddened. "She, I mean...we..."

"Nancy, you're making me nervous."

"W...why?"

"Because you sound as if something's wrong. Now where is Rasha?" His question held an insinuating tone.

"What do you mean where is she?" She said with disdain. How dare he even think about anybody other than her. "It's after midnight. The child is asleep."

"It's nine o'clock at night."

She glanced at her watch. He was right. She had been practicing her lies for so long, to use for the future, that she didn't have an answer for the present. This definitely put a dent into her plans.

"Where is she, Nancy?"

"I don't know." She sighed. "Let me go see." Instead of allowing him to wait on the line, she ended the call.

She had to collect the little bitch asap.

There was no way she could fake like she was missing if he knew. She had to pick Rasha back up, put the fear of God into her to keep quiet and then try another time. And so, she jumped in her car and headed back to the area she dropped her off. But when she returned, she didn't see the child. And since it was well after ten o'clock, once again she was greeted with some not so happy faces staring at her within the darkness.

Parking her car, she looked around from the inside.

KNOCK. KNOCK. KNOCK.

Rattled, she jumped in her seat when she heard the sound.

When she turned her head a tall young man with skin the color of milk chocolate was knocking on her window. He was dressed in all black and even in the night was a handsome and powerful sight.

"What do you want?" She yelled while trembling.

"You up?" He asked, referring to the drugs in his pocket. He may have put on like he didn't know her intent, but he was very smart.

"What?" She frowned. "What are you talking about?"

He laughed and then slowly allowed his face to crawl into a glare. "Why you drop that little girl out here by herself?" He asked in a deep voice. "Huh? Fuck is wrong with you, bitch?"

Her eyes widened. "I don't know what you're talking about."

He lowered his head. The window framed his face like a painting. "See my face?"

She nodded slowly.

"My name's Black Palmer. And if I find out you fucking with that little girl again, you gonna see me." He nodded toward the side of her car. "You gonna see my boys too."

"But I—."

He slammed the window with a full palm, causing the car to rock. "Do you understand me, bitch?!"

"Yes, yes, yes!" She wept softly. "I...I understand."

He rose.

And when she turned her head, she saw that the same men who in her eyes looked sinister in front of The Oxford, were now surrounding Rasha. She looked untouched. And unharmed.

More than anything she looked protected.

Nancy turned toward the stranger and swallowed. With a fake smile on her face, she said, "You ready to go home?"

Rasha just stared.

Black Palmer waved the men over. On gentlemen mode, one of them opened the passenger door and helped Rasha inside. Before closing it shut, Black Palmer said to Rasha, "If you need us, call."

She nodded and took time to remember each inch of his face.

He winked.

Rasha smiled.

When the chivalries were over, they closed the door and Nancy sped off into the night. If Nancy thought her troubles were over, she was mistaken. Because the moment she got home, Barbara was standing by her garage, with arms wrapped around her body. She was a slender white woman with beautiful silver hair and a firm stare.

More than anything she had a heart.

Once tucked in the garage, Nancy and Rasha piled out of the car. "Go upstairs, Rasha."

Rasha nodded. Before she entered the house, Barbara yelled, "Are you okay?"

Rasha turned to face her, nodded and walked inside.

Angry above all else, Nancy rushed up to her. "How dare you talk to my husband and my daughter without my approval."

"I know what you do to her."

Nancy stumbled backward. "What?"

"I said, I know what you do to her." She shook her head and looked up at the window. "I've seen how you overwork her body. I've heard how you yell at her when

Joe isn't around. Why are you so intent on creating a monster?"

Nancy turned red. "I'm not doing anything to her. And even if I were, it's my business." She looked her up and down. "All you want to do is screw my husband. That's why you told him I left with her isn't it?" She laughed. "Had you not been so nosey you would've found out that I dropped her off over a friend's house. And she—."

"Be careful with that child, Nancy."

"Meaning?"

"Like I said, I've seen her through your window. She's getting stronger. When she's older do you really want her as an enemy?"

Nancy was livid.

Her plan to get rid of Rasha was thwarted with people she didn't know were watching. With people who gave a fuck. And it didn't help when Joe finally called back early the next morning. She was lying in bed when his call came through.

BY T. STYLES

"Where is Rasha?" Was the first thing he asked. "I been calling all fucking night!"

She sat up in bed. "Wow. No good morning or —."

"Where is she?"

"I'll get her."

Before she handed Rasha the phone, Joe said, "I'll speak to her alone so you can leave the room immediately."

"Joe, this is silly." She laughed. "I won't —."

"Alone, Nancy!"

"Okay." Although she gave her the phone in her bedroom, she placed the call on speaker while she remained outside of the door listening.

"Rasha, Nancy told me you don't speak anymore." Joe said. "And that really makes me sad. I just want you to know that I'm going to be home soon. Do you hear me? I'm going to be home soon. And everything will get better. I promise."

The loving way he spoke to her, as if taking her side, sent Nancy on an additional campaign of anger. And so, it was time to try something new.

One day Rasha was coloring in her bedroom when Nancy entered. Lately she took to avoiding the woman at all cost, but it was tough since she lived in her home.

"What are you doing?" Nancy asked with her arms crossed tightly in front of her body.

She stood up slowly and dropped the yellow crayon. Why couldn't she just leave her alone? Why did she keep entering her space, when she made every attempt to stay out of her way?

"Were you in my cookies?" She stepped deeper into the room.

A head shake no.

"I don't fucking believe you!" She stepped closer. "Why don't I believe you?"

Rasha trembled and took one step back.

"You know how I feel about food don't you?"

She nodded up and down.

"If you eat, you have to pay your debt." She stepped back and pointed to the open door. "Go get on the treadmill."

Once in the home gym, Nancy closed the windows so that Barbara couldn't see, and she instructed her to walk first. And after some time, she increased the speed. As it stood Rasha had been running for two hours nonstop. Nancy was a horrible torturer. She had been going so fast, her heart beat out of her chest and she passed out.

Instead of leaving her alone, Nancy woke her up, fed her water and cookies that she didn't want, only to justify forcing her to run again. The stress on the young girl's body was astounding, and if the abuse continued, she could certainly die.

Feeling lightheaded, Rasha turned her head around to face Nancy who was sitting on the recliner. With wide eyes only she pleaded for her to allow her to rest.

Her voice remained silent.

"No." Nancy said simply as she sat in her chair and drank coffee.

Again, Rasha pleaded with her eyes, for just one ounce of mercy.

"No." Nancy took another sip.

With no choice, Rasha continued to run while fighting bouts of darkness that surrounded the outer edges of her sight. Her body felt heavy. Heavier than it had before, and her head felt wobbly. Within seconds, she could barely stand.

Although it was evident that Rasha was exhausted, Nancy was surprised at the strength she developed over the years. Why hadn't she collapsed and died already? She hated the child for being able to do for hours what she couldn't do for a few minutes. And so, her physical strength angered her even more.

Barbara was right.

Rasha was getting stronger.

After twenty more minutes of watching Rasha hold onto the handrails for dear life as her feet slammed into the treadmill, Nancy sighed. After all, it was she who was tired now, even though she was seated. "Ask for mercy."

Rasha continued to run, unable to fully understand what Nancy wanted from her.

"Ask for mercy, Rasha. Break your silence and talk, and I will allow you to rest." This was all a game to the woman, and it was evident in the way her eyes sparkled.

As Rasha's chest began to tighten and she found it difficult to breathe, it became clear that asking for mercy, would make her troubles go away. That asking for mercy, would make the pain stop. But, for some reason, despite her turmoil, she didn't want to say the words. She didn't want to give Nancy the satisfaction.

So instead of mercy, she found strength, and she would hold on to it with all her might.

Even if it meant her life.

Lying in a hospital bed, Rasha was awaken by a voice she recognized in the hallway. It was the sweet accented tone of Laurie, whom she hadn't heard from since she'd been fired by Nancy Hern. After a few more moments, she walked inside carrying a large red bag. But something was different. Laurie's energy was anxious. "Get up, bebe."

Rasha moved around slowly.

"Get up. Now!"

Rasha opened her eyes wider but remained lying down.

"We have to go! There's no time for delay." Laurie yanked back the sheets and then ran to the door to make sure no one was coming. Looking out of it anxiously, she returned and helped Rasha into a seated position on the edge of the bed. "Put these on." She dug into the bag and handed her a shirt and some jeans.

But Rasha remain seated, refusing still to use her voice. Not only because she made a vow, but also because she was exhausted after being admitted for cardiac arrest.

"Why aren't you talking?"

Silence.

Laurie took a deep breath. "Listen, I know you are upset with me. But you must understand, I would never leave you if I had a choice. You're like a daughter to me. And I'm so sorry that you went through what you went through alone. But I'm here now, and I need you to talk for me, bebe."

Instead of speaking, Rasha wrapped her arms around her tightly. And while Laurie appreciated the love, she needed her to understand the brevity of what was going on.

Grabbing her arms, she looked into her eyes. "Barbara called me when she saw the ambulance. She's worried and I have to get you out of here. Before Nancy finishes what she started. And this time there may be blood."

CHAPTER 3

SIX YEARS LATER

Laurie and twelve-year-old Rasha were walking down the steps of their apartment building when she noticed her sneaker was untied. Over the years, and without any healthcare, Rasha had changed for the worse. Her face was riddled with pimples and her teeth had begun to turn yellow and rot, causing her to feel and look ugly.

Despite the changes, she had yet to say a word. Instead she chose to voice everything with her eyes.

And they were indeed full of mystery.

Laurie and Rasha did everything together. Grocery store trips. Walks in the parks. They were inseparable, and as a result their bond grew heavy. And at the same time, they had lived in relative hiding. Because Laurie taking Rasha away from Nancy Hern, who was her legal guardian, was essentially going against the law. And both were worried that at some point she would return to take their happiness away.

Looking at her unlaced shoe, Laurie plopped on the step and pulled her toward her. "Give me your foot."

She positioned it in her hand, as if she were Cinderella.

"I thought I told you to tie your shoes when you were in the house." She looked up at her.

Rasha smiled.

"You could've tripped, Rasha." She continued to lace her sneaker.

Rasha scratched her scalp and then flung one of the two pigtails she wore over her shoulder.

Laurie shook her head. "I wish you would speak to me. After all of these years, why won't you speak to—."

Suddenly the building's door opened, and her next-door neighbor Bridget and her daughter Samantha walked outside. The moment Laurie saw the child's face, she seemed to brighten up and Rasha took notice.

Unlike Rasha, Samantha was a pretty girl, about ten, with long black hair that ran down her back. A mixture of black and white, to Rasha she resembled her favorite doll.

"Laurie, thank you for the gift." Bridget smiled and looked down at Samantha. "She loves it."

What are they talking about? Rasha thought.

Laurie cleared her throat, glanced at Rasha and looked back at Bridget. "I know what you're about to ask me and the answer is no."

"Please, Laurie. If I don't appear at work today, I'll lose my job. I really need you to let Samantha sit with you. Only for an hour."

"Appear at work?"

"Yes, um, I work on stage."

"Oh, I get it. Well I was just about to go to the market and —."

"Maybe she can watch her." She asked with wide eyes. "She's old enough."

"Rasha? But she never watched a —."

"I just need her for one hour before my real sitter comes."

"But she, she doesn't speak."

"She can't bring the chalkboard you bought her. To communicate?" She stepped closer. "I mean, what's the worst that could happen?"

An hour later, sitting in the middle of Bridget's tattered brown sofa, Rasha clutched the small chalkboard that hung around her neck, as Bridget ran about her apartment in a hurry. She had been given a cup of water, with extra ice.

"Don't worry, Rasha, everything will be fine."

Rasha nodded and burped.

"If you want to talk to Samantha, just write on your chalkboard and she'll get the picture. I promise."

Rasha smiled and then hid her grin to conceal her terrible teeth.

"The babysitter will be here in about an hour." Suddenly Bridget's eyes popped open as she scanned her apartment from where she was standing. "My keys, where are my keys?"

Rasha grabbed the yellow chalk on her board and wrote, IN YOUR PURSE.

Bridget scanned the board, dug inside her brown purse and snatched out her keys. She breathed a sigh of relief. "Thank you. You're the best already."

Rasha scratched her acne covered face and smiled.

Within seconds she was out of the apartment.

When the door closed, Rasha slowly walked toward Samantha's bedroom. Where she was sitting on the bed holding a doll. The same doll that Laurie gave her years ago, which up until recently, she deemed Rasha was too old to play with. It was the main reason she hid it in her closet, underneath her shoes.

So, that was the gift they were talking about outside.

For the first time ever, Laurie had betrayed her by stealing her doll and regifting it to another. She deemed that Rasha had gotten to obsessed with the toy, even though she was the one who gave it to her.

It was okay though.

Because it was time to get it back.

A snaggletooth frown covered Rasha's face which she quickly replaced with a smile. She wrote on her chalkboard, WHAT U DOING?

Samantha shrugged and gripped her doll tighter.

Rasha frowned, underlined the sentence and slammed an exclamation point on the end.

"Playing with my doll."

Rasha erased the board with her forearm and wrote: THAT'S MINE.

"But I want to keep it." She clutched it closer to her chest.

Erased. Wrote: THEN U HAVE 2 WORK 4 IT.

Slowly Rasha walked toward the dresser, grabbed the jump rope that was hanging over the mirror. Placing the chalkboard down, she swung it briefly and motioned for her to rise.

Not feeling much like jumping, Samantha shook her head no.

Rasha glared and clutched her fists tightly.

Knowing how mean she could get from when they played together in the past, slowly Samantha rose and placed the doll down on the bed as Rasha eyed the doll closely.

Grabbing the chalkboard, she wrote: JUMP. She flopped on the bed and grabbed the doll, stroking its hair.

Slowly Samantha complied, as she jumped in her small room. Slapping everything near with the rope in the process. When she saw the girl was tiring, Rasha wrote on her chalkboard: FASTER.

Samantha complied.

This was Rasha's first taste of mind games.

This was her first introduction on mental torture.

And she liked it.

Laurie walked through the door of her apartment exhausted after cleaning her last home for the day. She was responsible for fifteen, and the money was enough to stay barely above water. But when she got home,

BY T. STYLES

unfortunately she couldn't rest because Rasha required attention.

Using her chalkboard, she wrote: I MISS U WHEN YOU'RE NOT HERE.

"I know. But I have to work, bebe."

Rasha frowned.

"Bebe…" Laurie moved closer.

She nodded.

"I need to talk to you about Samantha."

Rasha crawled in her bed, tossed her chalkboard next to her and crossed her arms over her chest.

"What happened to Samantha? When you watched her at Bridget's apartment?"

Rasha sighed.

"Rasha, what did you do? Bridget says she doesn't want you babysitting anymore."

Rasha stared at her but more like she was staring through her, and it rumbled Laurie's soul. How could a young child look so evil?

"Rasha, I know you've been through a lot. But you have to —."

Before she could finish her sentence, Rasha jumped up and exited the room, leaving her alone.

An hour later, while Rasha was in the shower, Laurie began to cry in her own room. Normally she would move around the world happy, but it was mostly to disguise a deep sorrow that Laurie kept to herself. Choosing during her saddest moments to weep softly in her room to unleash the pain in her soul. So Rasha wouldn't worry.

Tonight, it didn't work.

Rasha walked through Laurie's open door and saw her on her knees in a tear-filled prayer.

Curious, she entered.

Laurie sniffled, stood up and sat on the edge of the bed. Reaching out to Rasha she said, "Come here, bebe." She wiped her tears with the palm and back of her hand.

Suddenly, Rasha ran out of the room, grabbed her chalkboard and reentered. Sitting next to her she wrote: WHAT'S WRONG?

"No, bebe."

WHY ARE YOU CRYING?

"I don't want you to—."

She angrily wrote on her board: U SAY WE FAMILY! TELL ME!

"I said no."

Rasha stomped her foot. When her towel dropped, she didn't bother putting it back on. Standing in the middle of the floor naked she wrote: IF U MY MOTHER. Y DON'T U TRUST ME?

Laurie sniffled, got up and grabbed one of her white oversize shirts from her drawer. Dropping it over Rasha's body, she quickly covered her frame. Pulling her hand softly she walked her back over to the bed where they sat on the edge. "My daughter is...she's...she's having trouble back home."

Her eyes widened. This was the first she heard of Laurie having a child and it tore her apart.

"Yes, bebe. It's true. I have a daughter."

She wrote vigorously, causing chalk crumbs to fall to her legs. U NEVER TOLD ME.

"I didn't tell you because talking about her hurts. It hurts bringing it up now. But...but I want to change the way I look at things. I want to feel the pain, because it reminds me that she's still alive."

WHAT ABOUT ME?

"Rasha, dear, I gave birth to her. And missing her doesn't mean I don't love you too."

WILL U LEAVE ME?

"Never!"

That was a lie to hear Rasha tell it. And she felt a rage inside of her body rumble. While Laurie spoke, Rasha took a moment to look at her smooth vanilla colored face. She wondered how it would look, if she etched small cuts throughout the flesh of her cheeks for hurting her feelings.

She wrote: I CAN'T LOSE U 2.

"You won't. Besides, my daughter and I will never be able to see each other again. She's in Mexico and with me cleaning homes, I don't make enough money to bring her here."

Suddenly Rasha smiled. If she couldn't get to America there was no need to consider her a threat.

"There's nothing I can do."

WHY?

"Because even if she can make it here through a coyote, I won't be able to keep her safe. Her life will never be enjoyable because she'll always be hiding. She will always be looking over her back."

Rasha looked down and wrote: LIKE ME.

Rasha thought about the strange woman who always seemed to follow her in the distance. She was certain that she worked for Nancy and was preparing at any moment to separate her from Laurie. She would never feel safe until Nancy was dead. Of that she was certain.

"Listen, I'm not hiding you. I just don't trust Nancy, even after all of this time. So, changing your hair, and trying to make you look different is for protection, that's all."

Rasha smiled. IS THAT WHY I CAN'T GO TO SCHOOL?

"Anything to keep you safe."

WHAT IS HER NAME?

"My daughter's name is Helena." She smiled brightly and looked outward. "And she's the prettiest thing I've ever seen in my life."

The chalk dropped from her hands as Rasha fell deeper into her feelings. Up until that moment, she always told her she was the prettiest thing. And she liked hearing it, even if it were all a lie.

It was Christmas eve and Laurie and Rasha had everything planned out for the day. For starters they would make cookies, prepare a small dinner and dance to holiday songs. Their meal was almost complete when Laurie grabbed Rasha's hand and pulled her toward the tree.

Looking down at her she said, "I want to talk to you for a minute."

Rasha rubbed her shoulders and Laurie, understanding what was said without words because she knew her so well replied, "I'll get your sweater for you in a second. I want to give you an early present first." She was so excited she could barely stand still.

Rasha's eyes widened.

"I know. I know what you're thinking." Laurie laughed. "I said no presents before Christmas but having you in my life has been such a blessing. And I want you to know how much I love you." She grabbed a small red and gold box from under the tree and handed it to her. "Open it."

Rasha ripped through the box so fast she almost destroyed her gift in the process. When she got to the center, she revealed a beautiful gold cross that dangled in her hands. It was large, but she would grow into it for sure. Catching the light from above, Rasha's eyes lit up she was so happy.

"Do you love it?"

Rasha nodded up and down rapidly.

"I want you to remember this whenever you feel alone. Whenever you feel as if the world is not on your side, hold this and remember its power. Because when you do, that power belongs to you."

Loving the gift, Rasha extended the chain and Laurie took it from her hands and put it on her neck. It was spectacular and Rasha ran her hand down the beautiful medallion. Looking up at her she sighed deeply and mouthed the words thank you without making a sound.

She kissed her on the top of the head. "Now let me go grab your sweater."

Rasha smiled, hopped on the sofa and looked down at the cross. She was in awe of its beauty. And while wearing it, she did feel stronger.

While she examined the jewelry in the living room, Laurie walked to Rasha's bedroom and into her closet. When she spotted the red sweater in the back, she paused when her toe brushed over something hard.

A doll's head.

When she removed it, she was shocked to see that it was the doll she had given to Bridget's daughter. So why was it in the closet? Taking it with her, she walked toward the living room.

"Rasha, what is this doing here?" She glared.

There was a smile on her face until that moment after getting the gift. But slowly it crawled into a frown as she looked at what she deemed was her property.

"Rasha, I asked you a question. Why is this here? I gave it to Samantha."

She grabbed the chalkboard and wrote: IT IS MINE. When she was done, she jumped up and snatched it out of her hand.

"Rasha, but I gave it to —."

Rasha erasing the board angrily put Laurie on pause. YOU HAD NO RIGHT.

"Rasha, you are wrong for —."

IT IS MINE!!!!!

Laurie was uneasy, and about to press the issue when...KNOCK. KNOCK. KNOCK.

"Who is that?" Laurie said mostly to herself. Needing to examine who was knocking on her door, slowly she approached it and looked out the peephole. Within seconds she stumbled backwards.

Concerned, Rasha ran to her side and held her hand. What could she do to help her mother? She looked down at her. More than it all, what was wrong. She'd never seen her in a broken down way in all of her life.

"I'm...I'm fine, Rasha."

KNOCK. KNOCK. KNOCK.

Pulling herself together, slowly Laurie walked toward the door and yanked it open. And when she did a beautiful fourteen-year-old girl rushed inside and wrapped her arms around Laurie's body. But someone else was present. In the hallway remained a tall Spanish man, with penetrating eyes. He was wearing a brown vintage style raincoat and he looked evil.

His words were simple but held weight. "You owe," he said with a booming voice. "Pay or you die."

Laurie closed the door and continued to hold her child. Despite the veiled threat, it was clearly the best day of her life. She prayed for this moment. She wished for it every day, but not once did she think it would come to pass.

But she was wrong.

"Mommy!" Helena yelled. "Mommy, I love you!"

Embracing her tighter, Laurie wept loudly as she held her only child in her arms. All while Rasha watched from the sidelines.

With malice in her heart.

It was raining outside…

Rasha was lying down, while looking across at Helena who was sleeping in her own twin bed. She had been sinking into a deeper depression ever since Helena showed up and she didn't see things changing anytime soon.

Before Helena came along, Laurie would make her feel like she was the only one. The prettiest girl despite her bad looks. And now, she was ignoring her in exchange for her trophy daughter.

Wanting to get a better look at the pretty girl, she eased out of bed and tiptoed across the room. Sitting on the edge of Helena's mattress, she stared at her beautiful sleeping face. She had a close view and proclaimed quietly that she was definitely the prettiest girl. The window was slightly open allowing the moon to shine through, and so she could see every detail.

If only she could look like her, maybe boys would notice her like they did Helena. If only she could be her.

Curious, she touched her hair. It was soft.

Then she sniffed her feet, her legs and even her vagina, before moving to her belly and neck. She was about to touch her when Helena jumped up and yanked the covers over her body.

BY T. STYLES

"What are you doing?!" She sat up in bed, her back pressing against the cool wall. Thunder ripped at the sky.

Rasha eased off her mattress.

"What were you doing, Rasha?"

Trying to prevent Laurie from waking up, Rasha hopped in bed, and pulled the covers over her head. But the damage was done. She had proven herself to be weird. And Helena was frightened to her soul.

Laurie and Rasha were making a big meal to celebrate Helena's birthday. Normally when they celebrated Rasha's birthday, the money would be low, but suddenly for Helena's Laurie was able to go all out.

Cake, food and gifts.

After all, Laurie for the first time had resorted to selling pussy. And she would do it again if she had to for Helena.

While Laurie was preparing the meal for the three of them, and Helena was combing her hair in their room, Rasha used the time to talk to her using her board.

AM I PRETTY?

Laurie glanced down at it quickly but focused back on the pots. "I don't have time to read your board right now, bebe."

Rasha walked around her side and held the board higher.

AM I PRETTY?

She sighed. "Rasha, not everyone can be pretty. Some girls gotta be smart. Some girls gotta take the first man who wants them. It doesn't make them less important. It just is."

Rasha was devastated.

She erased and wrote: HELENA?

Laurie shook her head. "She's the kind of girl who can get any man she wants. With looks like that she'll always be a weapon." She said proudly. "Now go grab the juice out of the fridge. Dinner is almost done."

With her world rocked, Rasha ran out of the kitchen crying.

2002

THREE YEARS LATER

BY T. STYLES

Time had passed and Rasha and Helena forged somewhat of a bond. But Rasha had other motives in mind. She wanted things to be the way they were before she arrived. And as a result, Helena didn't always feel comfortable around her when they were alone. One day she took to her mother about her while she was preparing Spanish rice for dinner.

"Can I talk to you, mama?" She whispered as she walked into the kitchen, looking behind her once to make sure Rasha wasn't coming.

Because Rasha was like a shadow.

Always near.

Laurie banged the spoon on the edge of the pot once, to kick the rice into it. "Sure, honey what is it?"

"Something's wrong with Rasha."

She smirked. "Why…why would you say that?"

"Sometimes she ignores me."

"Well sisters do that all the time."

"But this feels different. It's like when she doesn't want to see me, she acts as if I'm not in the room. And then when I get used to it, she looks at me and it…it…" She looked down.

Laurie walked up to her. "What is it, Helena?"

"When she finally looks at me, she scares me. She'll just stare at me when I'm in the bed, or when I'm sleep and not say anything. I think she hates me. It's almost like she's not the same person."

She giggled. "Oh, Helena stop it."

"Mama, it's not funny."

"I don't mean to laugh, Helena." She stroked her arms lightly. "But believe me, Rasha is harmless."

Helena looked down. "If you say so."

"I do. Trust me. Things will be fine."

"I hope so." She walked away with her head hung low.

Laurie didn't like her daughter's mood, and so she took her seriously.

A few days later Laurie was running around the apartment trying to get ready to leave. When she was finally ready, she walked into the room the girls shared together.

"Okay, girls, I have to go to work." Laurie said entering their space. She kissed Helena first and Rasha second.

And Rasha noticed.

Rasha always noticed.

"Stay in the house." Laurie continued, walking toward the door. "I don't want anybody to see either of you. We have to be more careful than ever."

"Mother, why do we have to hide?" Helena asked.

Rasha ran to her bed and wrote: WE WILL BE FINE.

Helena looked down and read the words on her chalkboard. "You're right."

"Don't worry, Helena. It won't be like this always." Laurie promised. "I'm working on some things as we speak." She looked at Rasha and then back at Helena. "Bye, bebes."

When Laurie left, Rasha slid out of bed and began to brush Helena's hair although she preferred if she didn't touch her so much.

"Oh, Rasha, I wish you could talk." She sighed.

Rasha smiled.

"I have so many questions."

Rasha grabbed her board. LIKE WHAT?

"Is it true, that if I get married, I can stay in this country? And they won't be able to make me go away?"

Rasha nodded although she didn't have the facts all the way together.

"I hope you're right. And once I'm not a virgin anymore, I can get somebody to take care of me forever." She pressed her hands together and looked upward. She was always so dramatic.

Writes on board: I'LL TAKE CARE OF YOU

"How?" She frowned. "Mama says you'll be going to stay with your people soon."

Rasha frowned. She had no idea what she was talking about.

"Yep, says your people will be coming soon and then it'll be just me and her." She swung her hair over her shoulder and then looked in the mirror. "Well she didn't exactly say those words, but it was close. I hope you like your new family."

Rasha backed up on her bed and flopped down. Nancy had shown her, her family while cruising through the violent streets of Baltimore, and she wanted no parts of it, ever.

Helena's eyes widened. "Rasha...are you okay?" She covered her mouth with both hands. "Wait, you didn't know?"

Helena got up from her seat and handed her the chalkboard.

"Talk to me."

Silence.

Grabbing her hand, she placed the chalk in the middle of her palm. "Write to me, Rasha."

Slowly Rasha wrote the words: WHY DON'T PEOPLE WANT ME?

Helena looked down. "I want you."

Rasha looked into her eyes. *Did she really mean what she said?*

"Really, Rasha. If I had it my way, we would be together forever."

Rasha began to write: I HAVE AN IDEA.

"Okay."

LET'S GO.

Thirty minutes later they were sucking on snow cones and walking through the mall. Every now and again boys would look over at Helena and smile. After all, she was stunning. And make no mistake, she enjoyed the attention.

The girls were night and day.

Helena had luscious black curly hair and butter toffee colored skin, while Rasha maintained a butter yellow complexion with horrible acne. Unlike Helena,

Rasha preferred her hair to be snatched back in a ponytail that swung every time she walked.

But it was Rasha's eyes that made her face. She had such control over her expressions, that she could change them on command. They could be kind. Loving. Angry. Serious.

And even evil.

After getting a few looks from a lot of boys, Rasha yanked her hand which startled Helena a bit. Writing on the board she wrote: BE BACK

Helena's eyes widened. "Where you going?"

She pointed to the chalkboard again.

BE BACK.

She grabbed her hand and walked her to a bench inside the mall. Erasing the board with her forearm she wrote: STAY. And walked away.

Almost an hour later, Rasha strutted up to the bench with a smile on her face, but Helena wasn't there. Moving toward the side door, she saw her leaning against the wall crying while she was sitting on the ground. Her hair was all over her head, and she looked like she'd been rolling around on the ground.

Rasha immediately rushed up to her and grabbed her hand, but she snatched away. Helena sniffled and angrily asked, "Where were you?" She stood up. "Huh? Where were you?"

Silence.

"Rasha, where were you?" She said louder.

She erased her board, but Helena snatched it away and tossed it on the ground.

"Fucking use your voice! Mama told me you could talk before. So fucking talk now!"

Slowly Rasha bent down, picked up her board and wrote: I DON'T WANT YOU TO DIE.

Helena was scared.

Was she saying that she was capable of killing her?

Carefully she roped her arm through Helena's and the girls took the long trek home. Every now and again Rasha would glance at her and pluck pieces of debris out of Helena's hair. And when she looked down, she noticed Helena's knees were scratched and bloodied.

Something dark definitely happened.

They were almost to their apartment when from a far, they saw Laurie being escorted outside with an officer on each end of her frame. Her wrists were handcuffed behind her back and her face was flushed from crying.

The moment she saw the girls in the distance, she made eye contact and shook her head softly. "Stay."

Laurie mouthed so that they could see her, but the cops couldn't hear her words.

"What's happening to mama?" Helena asked with wide eyes. This woman was her entire world. She couldn't lose her. They had been together less than five years. She needed more time.

When she moved to run up to Laurie, Rasha yanked her back to her side. On the board she scribbled: THEY WILL TAKE U 2.

When she looked as if she would run again Rasha briskly erased and wrote: STAY!!

Within minutes Laurie was taken away while Rasha held her as she cried in her arms.

As Helena watched the car disappear from site, Rasha wrote: DON'T WORRY. U STILL HAVE ME.

"Rasha, stop!" She sniffled and tried to prevent herself from going into deliria. But it wasn't working. Her nerves were bad. She wanted her mother and yet she was gone. "I need my mother! You don't understand!"

Rasha was beside herself with trying to get her to calm down. She wanted her to know that she could take care of her now. That she could do a better job than Laurie, if only she trusted her.

DID U LIKE MY GIFT?

She sniffled and wiped snot away from her nose. "What gift?"

I GOT U THE BOY

Helena's eyes widened and she stumbled backward. "A...a boy?" Her heart thumped in her chest. "The one...at the mall?"

She nodded yes.

Upon hearing the news, she turned around and threw up on the ground. Falling on hands and knees she said, "He...he raped me. He pretended he was going to take me on a walk and raped me behind the mall! Who does stuff like that?"

Rasha frowned, erased and wrote: DIDN'T U LIKE IT?

She clenched her fists together and yelled, "No! No, I didn't like it! How did you even get him to do that?"

Rasha felt stupid. She figured after she said she wanted to get a boyfriend and not be a virgin, that getting her the boy would make her happy. Now she was learning that she was wrong.

"Rasha, how did you get him to do that?"

She erased and wrote: SAID U WOULDN'T TELL. CAUSE YOU'RE NOT ALLOWED TO BE HERE.

Devastated, Helena cried harder and Rasha sat down next to her. Erasing her board like a mad girl, she wrote: I WILL TAKE CARE OF U. I PROMICE.

An hour later Rasha was warming up some microwave pizza when the phone rang. Helena was still in the bedroom after having cried herself to sleep. Although Rasha didn't talk, she picked up the handset. The automated voice said, "You have a collect call from the county jail from *Laurie*. If you want to accept press 5."

She did.

Laurie's anxious voice was on the other line. "Hello, hello! Helena is that you?"

Silence.

"Who is this?" She sniffled. It was obvious she had been crying. "Is this Rasha? Say something. Please."

Rasha looked behind her to see if Helena was coming. To answer her question, she knocked on the phone twice.

"Why would you do that, Rasha? Why would you tell the people that I took you away from Nancy? You know I was here illegally! Don't you realize I will never see my daughter again? Don't you realize they will come for you? They won't let you stay in that apartment alone! They will be back!"

Rasha smiled.

"Is this about, is this about me reconnecting you with your family? Because if it is, I was going to do it the right way, Rasha. But...but someone was coming around the house asking questions. And I was afraid. Afraid they would...they would find us all and separate me from my daughter."

Rasha glared.

"I was going to make sure you were in a place where you would have the best of care. But now...well now I don't know what will happen to you." She cried heavily. "I don't know what dark places the world will take you because they are sending me to Mexico. But please, bebe, if you ever loved me, leave my daughter out of it."

CHAPTER 4
SOME MONTHS LATER

Rasha could smell the dank odor of the other twenty apartments in the building, meshing together in the hallway as she waited with her social worker. The white doors offered a stark contrast to the black walls throughout the building, making things feel cringy.

The social worker looked down at Rasha when they approached number 34B. "You'll be fine. I know he wants to meet you."

Rasha clutched her suitcase which had the doll's head sticking from the zipper in one hand, and her chalkboard hanging over the cross on her neck.

"And I know you are afraid to meet your father, but people make mistakes, Rasha. And with Laurie kidnapping you, maybe he couldn't find you at first."

Placing the suitcase down she wrote: WHERE IS POPPA HERN?

Instead of answering right away, the social worker examined the chalkboard. Why doesn't she talk, since she was told she knew how? "I don't have all of those answers, Rasha. But this is the best place for you."

She erased with her forearm. I'M AFRAID.

"Don't be." She sighed. "Beauty lies in the unknown." She paused. "But Rasha, if you don't make it here, you will go to a group home. This really is the last stop. So be nice to people. Try not to cause trouble. This is your last hope."

When the door opened an extremely handsome, tall man with salt and pepper hair appeared. He smiled down at Rasha and the moment she saw his face, she fell in love.

He would be her new obsession.

"Mr. Dupree," Mrs. Sharpley started. "How are you?"

He nodded. "Is this her?"

It took a special kind of man not to know his own daughter's face, so the social worker was irritated and frowned. "Yes, sir, this is your child."

He nodded. "Ugly. Unlike her mama." He looked at her legs. "Built strong though." He licked his lips.

Mrs. Sharpley cleared her throat. "May we come in. I have some things to go over with you before I leave."

He opened the door wider and touched Rasha's long curly hair. Bending down, he brought a waft to his nose and inhaled. "At least she smells like peppermint."

The Social Worker frowned. "The child doesn't like sugar. Or candy of any kind."

ASK THE STREETS FOR MERCY   95

He nodded and observed her body closer. "I can see. She looks fit." He stepped back "Come inside."

Upon quick glance, the social worker approved greatly at how neat the living room was. It had an old feeling, no doubt, but at the same time everything had a place. There was a lot of wooden furniture and appliances. Even the kitchen had wooden cabinets, along with the floors. At the end of the day, the two-bedroom apartment seemed very country despite being in Baltimore city.

She waved really quickly and then said, "Sit down, Rasha."

Rasha obeyed by flopping on the sofa. Although she was compliant, the thing was, she didn't want to sit down. She wanted to take in the sights. She wanted to take in her new home.

The social worker walked up to Lester. "Can I see where she'll be staying?"

He scratched his beard and it crackled like popcorn. "Come with me."

When they disappeared into the back of the apartment Rasha could see twin beds in the room as they walked further inside. When they were gone, she took a moment to look around. Her eyes rested on some things longer than others because she had selective

BY T. STYLES

memory and selective focus, choosing only to recognize those things that created the picture she desired.

After a while, she realized what she already knew to be true. There were no pictures of her anywhere. It was almost as if she didn't exist.

Now she was angry.

Maybe she would use her voice and tell him so.

Even if it meant he would die.

When they came back into the living room, the social worker smiled at Rasha. "Well, everything looks good. I think you'll like it here. You'll have plenty of company."

Rasha nodded.

"Well, I have to go." She shook Lester's hand. "Call if you need anything."

He nodded, more eager for her to leave than anything else.

When she exited the apartment, he sat next to her really close. Rubbing her leg, he said, "You can't stand that stupid bitch either can you?"

Rasha blinked a few times.

"You and me are going to get along just fine. But there are some rules in my house."

She nodded.

"You do what I ask, no matter what. You don't make life for me here hard. You don't tell anybody what goes on inside of our apartment. And you never, ever touch my car." He moved closer. "Are we clear?"

She nodded.

"That's my girl. We belong together."

She smiled up at him with wide eyes because she believed it was true.

At midnight, Rasha snuck out of the apartment and then out of the building. She was wearing her chalkboard around her neck as always, a t-shirt, sneakers and jeans. When she turned left, Helena was waiting on the steps of another building. She was scared and trembling.

"What took you so long?" She said rubbing her arms. "You promised I wouldn't be out here by myself."

Rasha looped her arm through hers.

"Where am I going to stay?"

She stopped walking, stared at her for a few moments and wrote: I'M GOING 2 TAKE CARE OF U.

"But how? You're just a kid like me."

She wrote: TRUST ME.

Helena nodded, after all she had no choice.

Rasha linked her arms through hers again as they continued to walk, to where she didn't know. They were almost to the second block when all of a sudden, a forty something-year-old lady yelled from the steps she was seated on, leading up to a building. She was a black woman with long silky grey hair that ran down the sides of her back, brushing the concrete steps under her body. She looked mystical and both Rasha and Helena stopped walking just to stare at her dark beauty.

But the woman seemed to be gravitated to Rasha. "You look like trouble. I've been waiting on you."

A storm was coming…

But it didn't stop Rasha from wanting to remain outside sitting on the stoop of her apartment building. Besides, there was nothing to do in the house. She was already on her third piece of sugarless bubble gum, and the taste went from flavorful to a bland wax consistency in her mouth. She continued chewing just to have something to do.

When she felt what she deemed to be a raindrop on her face, she was preparing to go inside the building until she saw two characters staring at her from afar. She'd seen them before, but they never spoke to her once.

Just watched.

As if she was something to be viewed or analyzed.

One of them, the tallest of the two, was holding a camera. At first it appeared to be pointing her way. And then he lowered it when she glared.

Was he filming her? If so, why?

Slowly they walked across the street. Like two shadows moving in the opposite direction. She was intrigued, so she sat back down.

"You live around here?" The tallest one asked. He had dark skin and hooded eyes.

She nodded. Wasn't sure if she could trust him yet.

"What's your name?" The shorter one questioned, as he scratched his honey brown face that was riddled with freckles.

She wrote: RASHA.

"That's cute. Um, my name is Kadir." He said clearing his throat. "And this is my brother Nalo."

She bobbed her head like an apple and scratched her pimply face.

Y DO YOU STARE AT ME ALL THE TIME?

They looked at one another and laughed. She didn't like it. One bit.

"Ain't nobody staring at you, girl." Nalo responded. "Ain't even nothing to look at to be honest."

"Exactly. Have you seen yourself lately?" Kadir laughed.

She had.

And she hated her reflection.

WAS U TAPING ME?

"If I was, would it matter?"

Despite the slight tension, they continued to get to know one another. Each checking the other out. With time a connection brewed. Even the rain seemed to pause to allow for the meeting. Although it didn't mean that the storm was not on the way.

It just meant that for now, things were calm.

"You heard of Crystal Flynn?" Nalo asked.

She looked at them both and shook her head no.

They laughed, although she didn't get the joke. "You will."

She wrote: WHERE IS SHE?

"Dead." Kadir responded. "She used to live in your building before she died."

She frowned.

"Hold up," Kadir said pointing at her. "What apartment you live in?"

She shook her head no.

"Ain't nobody trying to rape you, girl!" Kadir said.

That was a strange thing to say, but she felt a bit comforted by it. So, she wrote: 34B

The brothers looked at one another. "You live with Lester?"

She nodded. At this point she'd been nodding so much, her neck began to hurt. WHY?

"That's our uncle." Kadir replied. "That's why."

Suddenly the danger that appeared to surround them blew away. Even their postures, weakened a bit. Did they have ulterior motives before realizing they were all related?

Maybe.

Only time would tell.

BY T. STYLES

Rasha was spinning by the door waiting for Lester to come home. She had hoped they would spend more time together, but it turned out that Lester was way busier than she could have imagined. And still, she desperately desired a father and daughter connection.

The girl needed attention.

She needed love.

And that made her vulnerable to the world.

She was just preparing to sit on the porch when her newfound cousins Kadir and Nalo knocked on the door. With a smile on her face she opened it wide.

"Coming out?" Kadir asked rubbing his hands together as if he had plans. "We gonna kick it at my crib."

Although she missed Lester, the brothers always had something going on and it made time fly by when her father wasn't there. Unlike others who pressured her to speak, they seemed to enjoy her silence.

And so being around them felt easy.

Over the weeks, they started spending more time together. It was a connection that wasn't built on a strong foundation of trust, but at the same time was growing. And there always seemed to be a mystery surrounding the brothers which for some reason she liked.

Mainly because they accepted her, and she needed to be seen.

"You ugly but you got some big pretty legs," they'd say. "You run track or something?"

She would shake her head no, even though she spent every night outside of the apartment, running around the neighborhood. She found comfort in jogging, feeling as if it made her stronger, quicker and more flexible.

More than anything she liked to observe people from a far. Often pretending to be them by moving her body like they did. She would do anything to live another life instead of living her own.

She would do anything to see Mr. Hern again.

During the night, she would also use this time to give Helena some food, who oddly enough had begun to stay with Sybil, the crazy old lady who lived down the block.

"Rasha, you coming out or what?" Kadir asked again while standing in the hallway. "Cause we ain't got all day."

She nodded, grabbed her jacket, and a brown paper bag before locking the door behind herself. On the way she dropped Helena's food off at Sybil's and followed them up the block.

As the brothers talked about any and everybody while videotaping the world, she sat back and watched. She observed the way they moved. The way they talked and the many people who spoke to them along the way.

Twenty minutes later they were in Kadir's and Nalo's basement playing video games. Their house was mostly a wreck, that refused to crash into itself, even though it should have a long time ago. It didn't make things better that their parents worked at night, leaving the boys alone to destroy the world.

Although Rasha never played the game before, she was a natural and that shocked them to the core.

Still, there were more pressing matters to discuss.

"Aye, Rasha, you want some sweet juice?" His eyes remained on the game the entire time.

She stared at the glass loaded with ice and red punch. "It's really, really good."

It looked good but she didn't like sugar. When she was younger, every time she ate sugar trouble occurred. And so she shook her head no. Besides, she could smell the liquor wafting from the cup. Her father kept a cup of something wet on the table regularly.

Taking a big sip, he put the cup down and continued to play the game. "You ever kissed a boy before?" Kadir asked.

Nalo looked at them both while talking to his girlfriend on the house phone. But there was only one thing that held his focus in that moment, and it wasn't his girl.

"Have you?" Kadir said.

She jumped up and looked for her board. As she was preparing to write on it, they rolled their eyes.

I'M ONLY 15. She showed them.

He smirked, shook his head and focused back on the game. "Damn, I thought you were a big girl."

I AM.

"So how come you never kissed anybody before if you such a big girl? Seems to me you would have kissed somebody by now. Maybe you're scared."

She shook her head no.

"You can try today if you wanna."

She frowned.

"He's not talking about you kissing us," Nalo said hanging up the phone without saying bye. He walked closer to the couch and stood over top of her.

He made her uncomfortable in the moment. I DON'T UNDERSTAND.

"I got somebody I want you to kiss." Kadir said. "To see how big of a girl you are."

Silence.

"Plus, I hear if you kiss a boy, it'll make you pretty." Nalo continued. "Don't you wanna be pretty?"

More than anything she did.

YES.

"So you gotta kiss my friends."

NO.

He glared because she was annoying. He had no idea such an ugly girl would be work, and he hated her for the rejection.

"Do you like hanging out with us?" Kadir asked.

She nodded yes.

"Then you ain't got no choice." Kadir said.

"Yeah, you gotta do it, okay?"

Twenty minutes later three of their friends, all around sixteen years old, were over the house. They all smelled of the outside world...like polluted air and sweat combined. Mostly because after getting the word that the brothers had a girl in the house who was willing to go "all the way", they ran over before the girl changed her mind. They were Avante, Baines and Greg. It could be said that the trio was attractive, but just like her cousins, something evil was all in their eyes.

"Are you ready?" Kadir asked as they began to surround her as she stood in the middle of the floor.

She wasn't ready.

She was horrified.

She looked at them all and moved toward the door.

When Avante reached out for her, she took off. Before she left out of the door Kadir said, "If you leave, you'll wish you didn't."

She left anyway.

When the door closed the boys were angry. Each of them had plans for what they were going to do to her, only to learn that it wouldn't go down.

"I thought you said she was with it," Avante said to the brothers, while groping his dick. Avante was biracial and wore long French braids running down his back.

Nalo shrugged as he wiped the sweat off his dark skin. "I thought she was with it too. I guess not though."

"Ya'll wanna see how far shit will go?" Kadir asked with a sinister smile on his face. "Because that bitch deserves to be dealt with since she playing games."

"You mean like we did Crystal?" Baines asked with raised eyebrows. He had brown skin and hair so fine and black it always looked wet.

Kadir nodded and grinned. "Yep just like Crystal."

"But Crystal died." Greg responded, as he wiped the sweat away from his light brown skin. "Or have we forgotten? Ya'll sure we should be fucking with this girl? I don't wanna go through that shit again. I mean she killed herself behind—"

"I'm sure," Kadir said. "And you can be with it or not. But either way it's getting done. Besides, I mean, what's the worst that could happen?"

CHAPTER 5

When Lester finally came home from work, Rasha wrapped her arms around him. Not being in the mood, he shoved her away and flopped on the sofa. The moment he did, she dropped to her knees and removed his work boots. She wanted to do something to prove how good it would be to have her in the house.

When he was settled, she wrote: WANT ANYTHING?

He looked at her for a moment, then looked past her, before focusing on her again. "Have Kadir and Nalo been near my car? I saw a scratch on it last night. And I know them boys like being around you." She looked around for the board and he grabbed her wrist. "Use your voice."

She shook her head no.

"Rasha, fucking talk to me."

Again, she shook her head no. If something happened to her father because she spoke directly to him, she would never forgive herself.

"Why?"

She looked at the hold he had on her wrist and he released her slowly. Crawling on hands and knees she located her board and wrote: BECAUSE I DON'T WANT TO HURT YOU.

He glared and stood up. "You know what, you're too weird for me." He shoved her to the side with his thick callused foot. "Stay out of my way."

Embarrassed by her father's rejection, and with her head hung low, she walked outside and flopped on the stoop. The moment she did she was greeted by a tall kid about her age. He had skin as dark as a black diamond, and a stab wound across the side of his face. He would be handsome if he wasn't so ugly. And yet there was still something about him that made her trust him more than anybody she met in the neighborhood.

Could it be a classic case of beast and the beast?

Instead of talking to her, he just sat on the step next to her and took in the sights. Loving his energy, she stared at him, observing him from afar.

"You smart for walking out on your cousins the other day." He smelled of the coconut butter his mother smeared on his skin, to heal the wound that would never leave. "They always be getting girls to do stuff."

When he moved to sit closer, she jumped back.

To make her feel better, he moved to a step further away. "I know I'm nothing to look at." He looked down.

"My dad not either. It's crazy cause my mother pretty like you. I wish I knew what happened to me."

Hearing she was pretty had awoken a place in her heart. And she warmed to him instantly.

She wrote on her board: U THINK I'M PRETTY?

"Yeah. Very pretty. And if you want, I can protect you. I can keep you safe." He smiled and she was surprised at how perfect his teeth were. "Maybe you can have my son when we get older. No pressure though."

She laughed before quickly hiding her snaggletooth grin. After all the man just said she was attractive. Did she really want to run him away?

"For right now, all I want is to protect you. From the boys around here. You need that right?"

She thought about the question. She was so busy trying to protect herself, what would happen if she had somebody do it for her?

"My name is Bezeno. But you can call me Zeno."

She erased with her ashy elbow and wrote: NICE TO MEET YOU.

From that point on the two were inseparable. And although he didn't look like much, she found comfort in him being around. What she liked about him the most, was that her chalkboard didn't seem to bother him. He accepted her form of communication and it made her accept him too.

If only she wasn't so bored.

Maybe it was a bad idea to be so mean to her cousin's friends.

Besides, they were cute. They were exciting. And all they wanted was a kiss. She remembered what Laurie said. Ugly girls needed to accept the boys who wanted them. Had she made a mistake?

One day she was sitting on the step with Zeno. Time flew by when she was with him because he always had a game they could play. He always had a nice word to say to her. And more than anything, he had dreams for their future.

Every day he would talk to her about what they would do when they were older. Where they would go and where they would live. He was convinced that she would bear him a son, and as a result, they would have this picture-perfect family.

Although she never used her voice, her elbow worked overtime erasing messages, confirming what he felt. Through time, Zeno had become consistent, and it was as if it were he and her against the world.

Maybe it was.

But evil works overtime in the life of the weak, if you let it.

One day she was sitting on the steps with Zeno when Kadir walked up to them. "What ya'll doing?"

She was shocked he even spoke to her again, since she knew he was angry about how she treated his friends.

On defense mode, Zeno rose and used his body to block him from her. "Leave her alone, man."

"Nigga, sit your bitch ass down," Kadir said. "That's my cousin."

Zeno could've dropped him but chose not to in the moment. Besides, based on how long they knew each other, technically they were friends. "If she your cousin, how come you ain't been back since you tried to let your friends hit?"

"I wasn't trying to let them hit." He looked behind himself and back at her. "I was trying to see if she was gonna do it. And since she proved she ain't no freak, I realized I like that even more." He focused on her. "You got a bathing suit?"

Her eyes widened and she shook her head no.

"I'll let you borrow one of my mothers. She a little bigger than you but it should still fit." He scratched his head. "But get this, we going swimming so come."

Zeno was annoyed. "Like I said, she don't need to go to no pool with you or your fucking friends."

He smiled. "How 'bout you let her answer the question for herself."

They looked at her.

"You rolling with me, cuz or what?"

Thirty minutes later Kadir and Rasha were at the community's indoor swimming pool. She couldn't swim to save her life, but she didn't want to tell him as he dragged her hand and pulled her into a sea of people splashing about like flopping fish in the water. Luckily at the moment they were in the shallow end.

At first anyway.

"You like it in here?"

She nodded as she tried to adjust the straps of the yellow bathing suit she was wearing. Kadir had tied it in a large knot in the back, but it was still falling off her shoulder, almost revealing her budding breasts. She felt some kind of stupid wearing it but decided to go with the flow. Besides, if she did, maybe his friends would like her. Maybe he would like her again.

"You look pretty."

She smiled. She loved to be called pretty.

"Can you swim?"

A head shake no.

"I'll teach you." He grabbed her wrist and tried to take her to the deeper end, but she began to flail her arms wildly, which caused a big scene.

Embarrassed, he yanked her toward him and said, "Calm down, before I hurt you."

Shivering she felt she better comply or else she would go under. Before she knew it, they were in six feet of water as he held her closely to his body. At least he felt warm.

Floating against the wall he said, "Just flap."

Her eyes widened.

"Your feet. Flap them."

Slowly she began to flap her feet but when she felt as if she were about to drown, she panicked, and he pulled her toward him.

Laughing hard he said, "I got you. I got you."

She was shivering she was so scared. Wiping the water out of her eyes, she did her best to see him clearly. Something told her she made a big mistake.

"Did I ever tell you, you had pretty lips?" He asked looking at her, and then past her before his eyes settled on her again.

She shook her head no.

"I want you to do me a favor. Okay?"

She shook her head no.

He glared. "You do it or I will let you go."

She shook her head no rapidly.

"You know what, get off me." He shoved her away and she flailed about as she felt her life slipping away from her. Water entered her nose, eyes and mouth and she couldn't breathe fully. When he felt the torture was sufficient, he prevented her from drowning by holding her against his body again. "Let me ask you again. You gonna do me a favor or not?"

She nodded and coughed repeatedly.

He smiled. "Good, I want you to hold your breath for five seconds. And then open your mouth."

She shook her head no until he stared at her seriously. After counting to five, she opened her mouth. A few minutes later she had done what he asked ten times.

"Good, now I want you to do it down there." Without giving her a chance to understand what was going on, he shoved her head under the water. While she was down, he undid his swimming trunks and tried to stuff his penis into her mouth.

She fought and threw her arms around, but nothing seemed to work. After being down for so long, suddenly she felt lightheaded. This appeared to be her last moment on earth. Seeing she wasn't fighting anymore, and afraid she had drowned, he released her and walked away. It was Zeno who dived into the water after her, after deciding to pop up.

Lifting her in his arms, he carried her out of the pool, throwing evil glances at Kadir all the way.

Rasha was lying on Zeno's bed watching a scary movie when he looked over at her and smiled. Tomorrow was Halloween and they decided to kick things off early. She was still thinking about what Kadir did to her at the pool, but she wouldn't allow herself to think about it long because it would make her cry.

Maybe he wasn't trying to kill me. She thought. She had plans to ask him later, so that they could be cool again.

When he continued to stare her down, she shook her head and focused on the television. It actually wasn't strange that he looked at her so often. Since they had gotten close, she always caught him staring at her and had gotten used to it. She was young but old enough to know that his was a look of admiration and so she loved it.

When he was staring too long, she grabbed her board.

WHAT?

He sat up on the bed. "Why don't you like me as much as you like other boys?"

She frowned. WHAT BOYS?

"Anybody but me."

With an elbow erase. She wrote: I LIKE U

"Not as much as you like them."

She rolled on her back and grabbed her board. I WISH U COULD B CUTE.

He looked down. "So you do think I'm ugly?"

DON'T U?

When they heard laughter outside of his apartment building, Zeno and Rasha rushed to his bedroom window. Down below she saw Nalo talking to a friend. The neighborhood was small, so it wasn't out of the norm.

When she grabbed her chalkboard and rushed toward the door Zeno grabbed her hand. "My mother is making us fries and hotdogs later. So we can—."

She could tell in his eyes he was hurt, but she needed excitement. And so, she snatched away and ran out the door.

When she walked outside, Nalo smiled and strutted over to her. "Hey, I didn't know you were in here." He hid the sun from shining down on his lying ass face.

"She at my house." Zeno said. Why couldn't them niggas just leave them alone? "We busy."

"Can I talk to my cousin alone?"

Bezeno remained and looked at her. He wanted her to choose him. He wanted her for once to send her cousin on his way.

Instead she nodded, essentially dismissing their bond.

When he left, Nalo said, "I never got the chance to say I'm sorry about what my brother did. Is it true he almost drowned you?"

She nodded yes.

"Stupid ass nigga. Well if it were me, I'd never treat you like that."

She smiled.

"What were you doing at Zeno's?"

BY T. STYLES

She wrote: WATCHING A MOVIE

"I got something even better for you to do." He smiled. "Want to roll with me?"

Twenty minutes later they were standing in front of an abandoned house. And she was barefoot per his request. The building was so broken down and barely staying in place. Its energy was so dark, she backed away from it slowly. That is until Nalo put his palm in the center of her back stopping her motions.

"Where you think you rolling to?"

She fumbled around for the chalk in her pocket. I DON'T LIKE IT HERE

She was about to run until he said, "If you want to hang with us you have to prove you strong. Plus, I can help get you closer to your father. I can talk to him for you."

She stopped and turned around. There was nothing more she wanted in the whole world than to be closer to him. And everybody in the neighborhood knew it too.

"But you have to go in there." He pointed at the dilapidated building.

She swallowed the lump in her throat. FOR HOW LONG

"Just two minutes. Just two minutes and it's all over."

Wanting him to help, slowly she trudged up to the house, pulled on the door and went inside. The moment she walked through the entrance, he shoved her deeper. It was so pitch black that she got dizzy and couldn't find her way around.

Running in circles, her heart beat out of her chest until she stepped on shards of broken glass. And still she didn't scream. But when she saw a figure in a white sheet, hiding in a corner, her eyes widened as she backed into a wall, had a panic attack and passed out.

When Rasha walked upstairs in her building with her father, by the way he gripped her elbow, she knew he was angry. The moment they walked into the apartment he laid into her. "The stitches in your foot cost me two hundred dollars. Fuck is wrong with you? I told you to be careful out here and that's what you do? Stay away from them stupid niggas or else!"

She wrote: I'M SORRY DADDY

"Fuck that shit!" He stepped closer. "If you keep at this weird shit you have going on, I will get rid of you.

Do you understand? I will get rid of you." He stormed into his room and slammed the bathroom door.

Rasha was in her bed the next morning when there was a knock at the front door. Embarrassed at what had been happening with her cousins, she had been crying all night. She waited for five minutes, before finally deciding to open the door. It was one of Kadir and Nalo's friends, Greg on the other side.

"Are you okay?" He asked rubbing her arms before walking inside without an invitation. "I heard about what happened and — ."

She pulled away from him.

"What is it?" He took one step back. "Wait, you blaming me for some stupid shit that your cousins did to you?"

Silence.

"So you're going to be mean to me?"

She looked around for her board and wrote: GET OUT

"What if I don't want to?"

He smiled, backed away and looked to his left. Sitting on the table by the door was Lester's car keys. Suddenly, he snatched them and ran out. Feeling as if she were about to die, she quickly followed.

As he ran around the car, she tried desperately to grab the keys back from him but

was unsuccessful. But when he slid in the driver's seat she slipped in the front seat and again tried to take the keys. It was no use, he seemed set on his plan to ruin her life.

"You're coming with me." He shoved the keys into the ignition and pulled off. "So you might as well chill."

Rasha was trembling as he sped down the highway, while driving the vehicle erratically. And without her chalkboard, she couldn't speak to him and so she had to wait and hope he wouldn't destroy the car and her life.

After ten minutes, he stopped in front of Avante's house and ran inside. She quickly exited the car and went after him. When he walked through an apartment door she never been into, she followed.

All she wanted was the keys.

Why were they trying to ruin her life? Was she that bad of a person?

When she did, she saw Avante sitting on the sofa eating popcorn with a girl. When he saw her, he stood up and faced her. "What you doing in my crib?"

Her mouth opened and closed.

"What is wrong with her?" The girl asked.

"She don't speak."

"I see that but why?"

"What you doing in here?" She looked around for a pen and paper and saw a 3-ring binder and textbook on the kitchen table. Walking toward it, she snatched a piece of paper and wrote: WHERE IS HE?

Avante looked at his girl and back at Rasha. "I don't know who you're talking about."

She wrote: PLEASE.

He walked up to her with a grin on his face. "Okay, it's like this, you do something for me, and I'll help you get the keys back to your father's car."

She nodded and wrote: ANYTHING.

Thirty minutes later Avante, his girl and Rasha were standing outside a shopping center mall. Inside were women's purses in a variety of colors. They seemed to bling while on display. "Go in and get that purse over there."

She frowned and wrote on the sheet of paper she carried. MONEY.

He smiled. "What you need money for when if you see something you want you can just take it." He stepped closer. "Just stuff it under your shirt. Nobody will know about it."

Silence.

"The purple one with the gold studs." The girlfriend interjected, while pointing over her head. "Now go."

Afraid, but wanting the car keys, Rasha walked into the store. In the beginning, the store employees were too busy with other customers to see her in the moment. Maybe she could take the purse without getting caught after all.

Slowly, she walked over to the purse and picked it up. It trembled in her hand until she put it closely toward her body and moved toward the door.

Looking out of the window she saw them staring at her with lowered brows. So she tucked the purse under her shirt and moved toward the exit. She was about to get away with it. She was actually about to get away with it. When she felt a hand on her shoulder, she turned around, only to see a tall black man with penetrating eyes staring her way. On the front of his black shirt were the letters reading **SECURITY**.

She was arrested.

As the police officer stood in the living room talking to Lester about her stealing from the store, she sat on the sofa trembling.

"I can't believe my daughter did this shit. I'm having a bad day. My car was stolen too," he said loudly, running his hand down the back of his head. It was the first thing she heard him say. "Who do I tell about that?"

"I'm here to drop her off." He pointed at Rasha with his thumb. "I'll send someone over later to take the vehicle report. I'm just here about your child."

When the officer left, he walked over to the sofa and stood above her.

She quickly turned to her left and grabbed her chalkboard. As the yellow chalk slammed against the board, it shook and fell out of her hand. Picking it back up she wrote: I'M SORRY. Erasing she wrote: DON'T SEND ME AWAY.

He smiled and sat next to her. "I didn't know you were into being bad." He placed a hand on her thigh and stroked lightly. "But now that I do, I'm gonna have to see what else you can get up to." He removed his hand.

"I have to get to work, but do you know anything about my car being stolen?"

She stared into his eyes.

Should she tell him the truth?

"Rasha, do you know anything about my car or not?"

Slowly she shook her head no.

He nodded, sighed and rose.

CHAPTER 6

Lester sat at the table waiting on Rasha to bring in French fries and hot dogs. When she brought the meal over, with the hot dogs already loaded with ketchup, mustard, relish and onions, he smiled. "That's my little girl." Earlier in the day his car was found in a ditch. And since he knew a body mechanic who would give him a kickback on the insurance payment to get it fixed, he was in a better mood.

She took a seat and grabbed her chalk board. I GRILLED THE BUNS.

He opened one of the hot dogs and grinned. It had a toasted color. "Yep, you sure did, my special girl."

A chair moved.

"So, how have things been?" He bit down into his hot dog. "You staying away from them niggas right? Because I'm still not convinced, they didn't steal my car."

She swallowed and nodded yes.

He frowned. "Why don't I believe you?" He put his hot dog down and wiped his fingertips on his shirt.

She slid her chalkboard across the table. PROMICE.

He frowned.

Looking at her chalkboard she rubbed the last two letters off and wrote: PROMISE

He nodded.

She grabbed her board and wrote: CAN I ASK QUESTION

"About what?"

She erased and wrote: MAMA

He sighed and sat back in the seat. Looking past her and then into her eyes he said, "Don't talk to me about that woman."

She looked down into her lap and fiddled with her fingertips.

He grabbed a toothpick and picked at his teeth. "I'll tell you this, she was pretty unlike you. And caused me trouble. And I was glad when she was gone."

She nodded and sighed.

"Loved her eyes. Loved her thick legs. Loved how good she smelled." He winked. "Reminds me of you."

She grinned.

"Now go bring me a beer." When she walked toward the kitchen. "Bring me two." He grabbed a fry. "Done got me all worked up for nothing."

She quickly fulfilled his request. And when she returned, he sucked one after the other down, until he was 'feeling good'. Standing up from the table, drunk and swaying he said, "Come over here. Dance with me."

A plate fell off the table.

She jumped up.

"Shut up!" He yelled. "Just, just shut up!" He looked at Rasha as she ran into his embrace. Turning the music on, at first, he kept her at arm's length. And then when the music slowed, he pulled her closer.

Closer than a father should be holding his daughter.

And yet Rasha was at peace. Because there was nothing that made her heart smile more than dancing with a father figure. She needed to connect to something, or she would be lost forever.

And he was giving her everything she desired in that moment.

When the fourth song came on, he was minutes from pulling her into the bedroom when there was a knock.

Angry at the interruption, he walked toward the door, opening it wide. It was Tiffany, his girlfriend. She was a thick, chocolate cutie with legs like a runner and an ass like a dancer. The woman was so bad when she was in his presence, he couldn't keep his hands off her. Without wasting time, he pulled her inside and kissed her sloppily.

Essentially forgetting all about Rasha.

Coming up for breath he asked, "What you doing here, Tiffany? Thought you couldn't hang out because you had to get up early for work in the morning."

She looked toward the table and back at him. "True. But I still wanted to stop by. I guess I missed you."

Rasha flopped in her chair, grabbed her board and wrote: DADDY!

He didn't even look her way.

Desperate in need for attention, she slammed the chalkboard repeatedly onto the frame. Still, his eyes remained on his girl.

As if she were not even a factor, they moved toward the bedroom door, but he stopped again. "Oh, I almost forgot, the day the police brought you home, you got a letter."

Her eyebrows rose.

"From a law firm."

She erased and wrote: 4 WHAT

"Open it to find out." They disappeared into the room and closed the door, leaving her.

Curious, Rasha rushed over to the counter and snatched the document. It was already opened so he definitely knew what was inside. Taking the letter, she walked outside and flopped on the steps.

This was the worst news ever.

After reading its contents, the letter floated out of her hand and fell to her feet. Suddenly there was a cool breeze on her back.

She glared.

And there was a breeze at her back again.

There was a reason to be upset. After all she just learned that Joe Hern had died. He was the last person she felt truly understood her. As she sat on the step, with tears streaming down her face, she felt stifled. For the first time since she lived with Nancy, she wanted to scream. She wanted to use her voice, but she couldn't.

"Are you okay?" Zeno asked walking up to her with his hands stuffed into his pockets.

She sniffled a few times.

Slowly he approached the steps and sat next to her. "Rasha, why haven't you been wanting to hang out with me? Why are you ignoring me?" He looked around and realized she didn't have her board to write down her thoughts. "Do you wanna come over my house and —."

She jumped up.

He was too annoying in the moment. With always trying to help her. So, she walked away, clutching her arms in the process. She was on her way to Sybil's house when a navy blue Honda pulled up alongside her. In the driver's seat was a man she didn't know. But in the passenger seat was Baines.

"Hey, pretty girl." Baines said with his hands on the window's seal. "Where you going?"

She looked at him and walked closer toward Sybil's, not wanting to be near any of her cousins' weird friends.

"I got some sweet juice," he raised a cup. "You want some?"

Ten minutes later she was in the backseat of the car while drinking juice loaded with vodka and sugar. It was her first taste of sweets since she left Nancy. Within five minutes, she was nodding off, while her clothing was being pulled off of her, one piece at a time. She couldn't tell who was doing what, but she did know this was not her plan.

Although she tried to fight back, her head was too heavy to see what was happening but the pain she felt between her legs ripped at her soul. Lying on her back, she noticed that the sun had gone down, and the moon had taken its place. To escape from what was happening to her body, she chose to focus on the stars instead. Before long, what she was enduring was so excruciating, she blacked out.

When she opened her eyes the next morning, she was no longer in the backseat of a car. Instead, she was

BY T. STYLES

lying on a damp patch of grass by a dumpster, her clothing sitting at her feet.

When she realized she was naked, she hopped up, got dressed in soiled clothing and ran home. Getting home felt like forever and when she looked down, she saw dried blood between her legs and slammed her hands over her mouth to stop from crying. Her life was going from bad to worse.

Right before she got home, she was shocked to see the police in front of her house talking to Lester. This was the worse-case scenario. They would take her away she was certain.

Backing away slowly, she ran in the opposite direction, before long she ended up at Zeno's house.

Knocking on the door hard, when he opened it, she wrapped her arms around his body and cried without making a sound. He picked her up, kicked the door closed and carried her inside.

Zeno was a gentleman.

And she needed that more than ever.

First, he ran her a bath and placed her carefully inside. As she brought her knees toward her body, he rinsed the blood off of her flesh as the water turned to pink. "Who did this to you?" He asked.

She turned her head away from him and laid it on top of her knees.

"Hold up a sec." He exited the room and returned with a notebook and pencil. "Tell me, Rasha. Who did this?"

She looked at the sheet and shook her head no. She simply didn't feel like writing or communicating.

"I understand." He washed her up again and said, "Oh, I almost forgot." Opening the book, he removed the letter that she left on the steps. He had picked it up when she walked over yesterday, figuring it was important. "This says you need to call the office. It sounds like this man left you some money. Don't you want to see what you're due?"

She didn't.

She wanted to be left alone.

Instead, she buried her forehead on her knees, and he tossed the book down.

Sitting on the floor, he rubbed her back. "You don't have to talk to me. Just, just know I'm here, Rasha. No matter what I'll be here for you. Even if, even if you don't like looking at me."

BY T. STYLES

Zeno had convinced his mother to let Rasha stay over for a few nights as long as he slept on the couch. She agreed. However, when his mother was in bed and awake, he honored her request. But when she was asleep, every night, he crawled in bed behind Rasha and held her as she cried in his arms.

His love for her was singlehandedly bringing her back to life.

While the window was open, he reminded her about how strong she was. About how beautiful she was and how she could do anything. It no longer bothered him that she found him unattractive. And she was happy to be in his life.

Grabbing a pencil and notebook she wrote: I WANNA HAVE YOUR SON.

His eyes widened. "For real?"

WHEN WE OLDER. IF YOU WANT ME TO.

It was the first time she had written since she'd been raped.

He held her in his arms where she fell asleep. Peacefully and at ease. The comfort she felt around him couldn't be put into words.

One morning, after he loved on her so hard, she woke up in a good mood. They were eating cereal at the table when she dragged her notebook and pencil closer. HAVE U SEEN MY FATHER

He sat next to her. "Yeah." He looked into the bowl of cereal, unable to face her head on because the streets talked, and he had listened.

Her eyebrows rose as she sensed something was wrong. WHAT?

He pushed his bowl to the side. "I think he went to see your lawyer. They saying he tried to get the money the man left without you. And he found out you can't get it until you're eighteen."

Suddenly her stomach twirled. She wrote: WHAT HAPPENED

He sat back in the chair and it squeaked. "I don't know. Want my mother to call your lawyer?"

She shook her head no.

Zeno sighed. "I forgot to tell you, I'm going to a party tonight."

Her eyes widened and she wrote: WHAT ABOUT ME

"I'm only going for a minute. Won't be long."

WITH WHO?

"You don't know them. It's up the block. Like I said, I won't be out long. I promise. Try not to worry."

She nodded.

He kissed her on the top of the head as they continued to eat their breakfast.

The hours ticked by slowly.

With Zeno's mother being gone, and Zeno being at the party, Rasha was bored. And so, she decided to see where he went. It didn't take her long to get her question answered.

Walking down the street she found the location immediately. But when she realized the party was at her cousins' house, due to seeing the flashing lights from his living room window and hearing the boom from the radio, she felt gut punched by Zeno's betrayal. Why did he not tell her he was hanging with her cousins? Especially after what they'd done to her over the past few months.

She needed answers.

She wanted to see his face.

Maybe he wasn't there after all.

So, slowly she walked toward the music and into the large door before disappearing inside.

ONE HOUR LATER

Rasha came bolting out the door yelling and flailing her arms from left to right. Not even a second later, Zeno came rushing out behind her, trying desperately to catch her. But having run all of her life, she was too fast and so, she had gotten away.

Sybil's apartment was a sight to see. There were plants in every corner of the room, and variations of dream catchers placed throughout the walls. She was a spiritual woman, who seemed wise to those who spoke

BY T. STYLES

to her for more than five minutes, but crazy to those who saw her in passing.

The way she made money didn't make things better and only added to the suspicion and the whispers around the neighborhood. Although most of her body had fallen in line with her age, her feet were dainty, cute, and tatted up with colorful flowers. As a result, she ran a very successful foot fetish business, in which she would charge men and women, to do whatever they dreamed to her feet, just as long as it didn't involve pain.

When Rasha first solicited her to let Helena stay in her apartment, Helena was afraid of the woman. Besides, she didn't know her well. But after a few nights on the street, she realized having a place to stay was better than having nothing at all. Within time, she and Rasha both gravitated to Sybil's confidence because she appeared to find a rhythm in crazy, that made her powerful.

After leaving the party hysterically, Rasha sat on Sybil's couch, shivering. She had given her warm clothing and a sheet of paper to write on.

I'M GOING TO MAKE THEM PAY. After showing Sybil, she tossed the paper down and rocked back and forth.

"Tell me what happened, Rasha."

ASK THE STREETS FOR MERCY   141

NO.

Sybil walked over a cup of tea to her and sat in her large green recliner. "If you hold a grudge, you won't live to see my age. Go to the police. Call your caseworker. And then when they are arrested, let it go."

Rasha shook her head no and glared.

She sighed. "I've seen your future, girl. And I'm here to tell you, if you go down this route, you will collect karma. And those of us who collect karma must pay."

Grabbing the paper she angrily wrote: WHAT ABOUT U? AND HOW YOU MAKE MONEY?

Sybil chuckled. "You say that to me as if it's an insult. She laughed harder. "Where is the crime in my line of work? I have a service, they have money, and we mutually agree to patronize each other." She lowered her head and began to rock in her chair. "But what will happen to you if you don't let this go will be much different. It will consume your life. Because grudges are greedy things and they eat souls."

U DON'T KNOW WHAT HAPPENED.

"Tell me."

"Rasha, I—."

She angrily wrote: MERCY.

"What's that?"

She wrote: MY NAME. AND I WILL MAKE THEM ALL BEG FOR IT.

Sybil sighed. "Okay, well, Mercy, I have done many things I'm not proud of. Things that I wasn't able to let go in enough time, and so it sits with me a bit longer. Because of it, you are my karma."

She glared.

"I knew it from the moment I laid eyes on you. You stayed in my dreams before I saw your face. And I mean to pay out my debt to the world, even if it means inviting the evil into my home. But once my debt is done, I will rest easy, knowing that I did right my wrongs. But you will never truly recognize love, even though it has already found you and will be the reason you die."

Rasha jumped up and bent down to grab her paper. She wrote: YOU DON'T KNOW WHAT I'VE BEEN THROUGH!

"You were hurt. I understand. I was sold to pedophiles at ten years old. So, I get it. But what about the people who helped you along the way? Call the police. Tell them what happened to you and then let it go. I'm begging you."

There was a knock at the door and Sybil frowned. "You expecting company?"

Mercy smiled although there was also pain in her eyes.

Slowly Sybil walked to the door. When she opened it wide, she saw a handsome man pulling on a rubber band. Behind him were two other men, leaning on doors within the building.

They looked serious.

"Who are you?" Sybil asked.

"Black Palmer." He nodded toward Mercy. "And we came for the girl."

Mercy walked to the door slowly. It was a reunion. The handsome stranger was the same man who saved her many years ago when Nancy threw her out of the car. Looking back at Sybil Mercy wrote: I'LL C U AGAIN

With that she walked out and got into their car that pulled away.

When they arrived at Black Palmer's place, he made sure that Mercy was comfortable at his apartment in The Oxford. They may have lived in the projects, but she was

144   *BY T. STYLES*

surprised to see that their living conditions were nothing like Nancy told her. Inside of their home was neat and clean, and everything had its place.

But it was the man who made her feel at home.

Under his watch she felt at ease.

Under his wing she felt more at home than she ever did, even at the Hern's. The thing was, it wasn't just him. It was as if everybody wanted her there. Black Palmer and his family not only showed Mercy love, but they opened up their hearts and what little they had, they gave it to her freely.

Later on that night, as she was tucked in bed he walked in the opened doorway. "Who was the woman you had call me?"

She grabbed her board. A STRANGER

He nodded. "I don't know what happened to you since the last time I saw you. But I want you to know that I'm here for you now."

I WILL ALWAYS REMEMBER YOU FOR THIS

He sat on the edge of the bed. The way he looked at her was different than any man had in the past. It possessed a quality she couldn't put into words. It wasn't lustful. It wasn't sneaky. It was genuine concern for her well-being.

"The one thing I want to know is, why you still don't talk?"

She shook her head no.

"Why don't you talk to me at least?"

BECAUSE I LIKE YOU.

As the years passed with her living with Palmer, Mercy became knowledgeable in the workings of street life. She learned the importance of watching her surroundings. Of not trusting everyone simply because they smiled in her face. Black Palmer wanted her to be a predator, never a prey. And since she knew what that felt like after being victimized all her life, she took his lessons to heart.

But she never got over the people who took advantage of her, despite being surrounded by love. Everybody at the Oxford's cared for Mercy. Black Palmer's friends. His mother. His aunts. His uncle's. They embraced her as if she were their own, and still she wanted for revenge.

The day she turned eighteen, everything changed. It was the day that she and Palmer made love for the first time. Since her first sexual experience was a rape, she was afraid and timid. He quickly put all of her fears to bed.

Lying on a bed of silk sheets, he was slow, sensual and attentive. Each of his touches were electrifying and sent chills up her spine in ways she didn't think were possible. With him she experienced what it meant to be wanted. With him she experienced her first orgasm.

As an adult, her life did normalize somewhat. She went out to eat. Went to the movies and did things she never experienced before. But still, the desire to seek revenge marinated in her soul and it quickly became the only thing of importance with the exception of Black Palmer.

It was a rainy day when Mercy and Palmer showed up at the lawyer's office dressed in all black. Because they were a power couple, which meant they would always be protected, the parking lot was littered with Mercy's squad whom she affectionally referred to as The Oxford Crew.

The fact that Mercy was a millionaress was a shock. Black Palmer had only learned a week earlier that she was wealthy because for him it was never about the money. It was about making sure that the look he saw in her eyes when she was thrown in the middle of the road would not be her story.

"Who are you?" The lawyer asked when Black Palmer stood at Mercy's side, with his arms behind his back.

"Does it matter? She signed the proper paperwork. So, we are here for what's rightfully hers. Now cut the damn check!"

A million dollars richer, the first thing Mercy did was invest into Black Palmer's drug business. She never considered herself to be a criminal. And it wasn't her original aim. But for what she wanted done she knew a million was only the tip of the iceberg. She needed millions, which meant a flip would be necessary.

Revenge was an expensive game, but she would bet the world to see it realized.

And that's exactly what happened.

A year later, when business was booming, Mercy wrote: BRING ME SYBIL.

For the evil she planned to pour onto the streets, she didn't want anyone bothering the woman she had grown to both love and be annoyed by.

"I'll send them now," Black Palmer said, knowing that although Mercy rarely showed affection, if she wanted the woman to be protected, she must have been important and so, that meant she was important to him.

But the mystic wouldn't go easily.

The moment The Oxfords arrived; Sybil gave them the business. "What are you doing at my fucking house?" She yelled at them. "I'm not leaving my home," she continued. Still, not one of them listened. Instead they entered and exited the apartment while removing her things in the process.

"I don't want to hurt you," one of them said. "But Mercy gave us orders, and we intend on seeing them through. You're coming with us."

She could see in his eyes along with the men who came and exited that there was no use in fighting. She would either relent or get snatched kicking and screaming.

"Well, where are we going?" She asked folding her arms over her chest.

"You'll see."

The moment she was brought to the sprawling property in Pikesville, MD, that was surrounded by an iron gate with the words MERCY spread across the front, her breath was taken away. She knew the evil girl would be powerful later on in life, but she never imagined it would happen so quickly.

The moment she walked across the threshold of the mansion, Mercy and Helena were eager to greet her. But it was Mercy who held a sign that read: WELCOME HOME.

Sybil wanted to be angry, but when she looked up at the cathedral ceiling, the crystal chandeliers and down at the marble floors all she could say was, "God, please forgive me, but I can get used to living here."

Helena laughed and Mercy winked as they showed her to her bedroom.

For a while things were calm in Mercy's mansion, and Black Palmer, The Oxfords, Sybil and Helena fell into the comfort of their new surroundings.

But Mercy never forgot.

Mercy never forgave.

Having some things on her own mind, one day Helena walked up to her while Mercy was lying on her massive bed looking at television. Clearing her throat, she said, "Are you still angry with me about what happened?"

She grabbed her board on the bed and wrote: SHOULD I BE?

Helena sighed.

WHAT DO YOU REALLY WANT?

"Mercy, I need my mother to be brought back from Mexico. It's my fault she's there and I am dying inside.

You have the wealth now. And. The power. Please don't—."

SHE BETRAYED ME.

"I'm sorry."

She erased and wrote: AND SO DID YOU.

Helena looked down. "What can I do to make things right? To bring her back?"

ANYTHING I ASK.

Kadir and Nalo were having sex with the same girl in Nalo's nasty bedroom. They were bottom feeders of the city and didn't care how gross they were. Everything smelled of piss and weed smoke in the apartment and it was evident that any self-respecting bitch would want no parts of either of them.

Luckily for them both, Rochelle was a dirty whore.

Kadir was hitting her from behind while Nalo had his hands behind her head as she deep throated his penis. They were getting it in good. There was long strokes from the back and wet sucks from the front but the oddest part of it all was that the brothers seemed more excited to be in the room with one another than they did to have the girl in their bed.

And yet, neither of them knew that their lives were about to change.

With no more than a wrist pop, within five seconds Black Palmer, under Mercy's direction had broken inside of their apartment. Stepping over trash, the living room was just as gross as the back and the smell made many of The Oxford's sick to their stomachs. But there was work to do.

Pointing at the cabinet under the TV she was certain what she was looking for would be there.

It was.

Tucked under the video games, were many home videos of women who didn't know they were being taped. Some were labeled, others weren't and so she took them all.

An hour later Mercy and Black Palmer stood before two police officers named Miriam and Watkins. This job was strictly business. Luckily for Mercy, Black Palmer had some dealings with the two men before and knew they would have no problem, for the right price anyway, taking Kadir and Nalo down.

After showing them the videotape of the young girl Crystal Flynn, who was gang raped by Kadir, and Nalo, the officers sent a squad car to pick them up. The case was major because when Crystal went to the police to tell them about the rape, no one believed her. Besides, she had been very promiscuous. And they had many tapes with her giving her approval of other sexual interactions. But this tape was proof, and had they had it before, she may not have taken her own life.

While they were dragged outside with their hands cuffed behind their backs, wearing nothing but boxers, they were angry when they looked to the right and saw Mercy standing next to Black Palmer and five other people they didn't know dressed in all black.

They knew she wanted revenge, but they never realized she was fully capable. As she watched them being stuffed into the car she wrote: DO EVIL MEN BREED EVIL CHILDREN?

He shrugged. "I'm a killer. And my father was too. So, you tell me."

Lester was on his fourth beer when there was a knock at the door. A little off balanced he opened it without looking out the peephole. It didn't matter because when he did open the door, he loved what he was looking at on the other side. After all it was his daughter whom he lusted after for the longest of time. Mercy was wearing a black raincoat and a smile, and the woman looked stunning.

"Wow, it's good to see you." He licked his lips. "Glad you decided to come home."

Silence.

"Let me guess, you still don't talk."

She laughed softly. "I only talk to those who need to hear my voice."

"And I'm one of the lucky ones I see." He smiled. "I'm shocked. Your voice is seductive. You sound just like your mama." He looked her up and down. "So, tell me, what you got under that coat?"

"Do you really want to know?"

His dick hardened with anticipation and he stroked himself to a full hard on. "I need to know."

"Then let's go find out." She nodded toward the bedroom and he rushed inside immediately, hoping she wouldn't change her mind. "Lay down." She instructed.

He complied and the moment he was flat on his back, she dropped her raincoat. Although she wasn't completely naked, she was definitely close enough.

154   *BY T. STYLES*

Wearing a black corset, black crotchless panties with garters connected to fishnet stockings and black pumps, she looked like she was preparing to go all the way.

"Close your eyes." She said in a lustful voice.

"Okay, okay, you're really getting into this aren't you?" He said stroking himself. "I'll play along."

The moment he closed his eyes she tiptoed out the room. When she returned, she had four Oxfords with her. They immediately held his legs and arms.

"What's going on?" He said anxiously as he watched his life flash by. "What are you doing?"

"You never cared about me." She said calmly. "You never cared about anybody. So why should I care about you now?"

"Please don't do whatever you're about to do. I was just playing with you. I wasn't about to fuck my own daughter."

"Sure you were."

Walking to her coat, she removed a blue latex glove. Sliding it on her hand she walked to the end of the bed. At first, she inserted one finger into his asshole, and then she inserted two as he cried out in pain. When he got louder, an Oxford slammed his hand over his mouth and then things got brutal.

Using her fist, Mercy jammed repeatedly into his hole, until it was covered in blood. He made every attempt to wiggle away from her grasp, but it was no use. The men had firm grips on his limbs. When she was done causing him extreme pain, she removed her hand and rose.

"You were right." She said softly. "I am daddy's little girl."

Walking to the head of the bed she slit his throat.

Killing him was her first taste of blood. But it wouldn't be her last.

Avante had gotten word that Rasha, who he found out now went by Mercy, was after all those who wronged her, and his nerves were on edge. When he first met the girl, he had no idea that she could be so vengeful. After all, she seemed innocent. She seemed harmless. And as a result, he underestimated her.

Within a matter of months, all of his friends were going down around him. A crew that was once tight had fallen apart. Kadir and Nalo were in prison for the rape that led to Crystal's suicide. Greg and his family moved away. And Baines seemed to disappear off the face of the earth. He was the only one who couldn't find shelter from what was coming his way.

And so, he went to the one place he felt she wouldn't be able to find him.

Knocking on his uncle Carlos's door, he was relieved that he agreed to let him stay with him for a little while. It wasn't like his uncle had the best living conditions. After all he was an addict. But it was better that he hid in a place where he normally wouldn't go instead of her finding him out in the open.

"Thank you for letting me stay here." Avante said as he locked the door behind himself.

"You my nephew. You can always stay with me." He flopped down in a cream recliner that was stained in the seat area. "So, what's going on that has your nerves rattled?" He stuffed a crack pipe.

"Nothing, I'm going to be okay." He sat on the sofa.

"That's not what I asked, nephew. It's obvious you're running from something if you're coming to my house. I just want to know what it is."

Instead of being comfortable, Avante's nerves were getting triggered over every noise outside of his home. Had he known it would be so noisy in his neighborhood, he may have stayed on the street, behind a dumpster somewhere.

"I did something a few years ago and now somebody won't let it go. It wasn't even that bad." He looked out the window. "It's like she—."

"Hold up, you running from a female?"

He nodded yes.

"Sounds like you're in big trouble. Don't nobody on God's green earth do a better job at getting revenge than a woman." He pulled the pipe. "You want some of this?"

"Naw, man!" He walked toward the window and looked out of it. "You know I don't smoke that shit!"

"Suit yourself. But it'll make you feel good."

When he saw how the drug appeared to alter his uncle's mood, he decided to give it a chance. It didn't take him long to fall victim. As the smoke coursed through his lungs, he realized he liked it. And just that quickly, he had given up on life, choosing instead to allow the drug to overcome him.

As the days went on Avante grew deeper and deeper into a drug habit. His old friends became a thing of the past and in their place came a new batch of people who held no morals or love for life.

Per the plan, a month later Mercy showed up at the uncle's house when Avante wasn't there. As they agreed on weeks earlier, she handed him a stack of money for his efforts.

"Wow, I ain't think you would really come back."

"I pay my debts. Always. You just keep doing what you're doing. I want him to become the grime on the streets."

The moment he heard her voice he trembled.

He learned from the streets that Mercy only talked directly to, those who she meant to kill. So, did that mean she wanted him dead?

"I thought you, I thought you didn't talk to people unless you were going to kill them."

She smiled. "You're already dead." She looked at the pipe on the table and walked away.

Mercy was angry when she showed up at Nancy's place, her old childhood home, only to find out she moved. As she stood in front of the brownstone, she was reminded of everything bad that happened in her life.

And still, she wouldn't feel at peace, until she got revenge.

When Black Palmer pulled up on the curb, and eased out of the car, she turned around and looked at him. Removing her phone from her pocket she texted: **HOW DID YOU FIND ME?**

He looked at his phone, "This is where it all started. So I knew you would be here."

She sighed and texted: **SHE MOVED. I SHOULD'VE COME HERE FIRST. NOW THE STUPID BITCH GOT AWAY.**

He nodded. "At least you found Avante."

She nodded.

"Why didn't you finish him, baby? Why you dragging this shit out?"

She sighed.

DEATH IS TOO EASY. I WISHED SOMEBODY HAD PUT ME OUT OF MY MISERY WHEN I WENT THROUGH MY WORST DAYS. I WANT THEM TO FEEL WHAT I WENT THROUGH. NO ESCAPING.

He walked in front of her and stroked her shoulders. "When will enough be enough?"

She looked down.

He raised her chin. "Are you saying never?"

She nodded at the house and texted: **IT'LL BE OVER WHEN I FIND HER.**

He read the message. "How come I don't believe you?"

PAY ATTENTION

By T. STYLES

CHAPTER 7

FIFTEEN YEARS LATER

Nancy shivered as she rode in the back of the silver Aston Martin. Despite the beauty of the vehicle, she was certain she was going someplace dark. After all, she had been snatched from in front of her home in Virginia, for reasons unknown.

When the car pulled up to a black gate with the words MERCY written in gold in the center, her heart dropped.

Upon reading the word, she had an idea who was behind the iron wrought gate now. And she was certain she was seeing her last day on earth.

When a tall black man with silver tipped dreads yanked her out of the car, she tried to smile, even though she was nervous. "Can you tell me how's Rasha doing? Because she's...she's in there right?"

Immediately the man stopped. "Never call her that again. Do you understand?"

"Yes, yes, of course," she nodded.

When they walked inside of the mansion, there was a black velvet king's chair outlined in silver in the middle of the floor. Surrounding it were The Oxfords.

The members were formed by those who lived in the apartment building that saved Mercy's life when Nancy left her to die.

Which ironically enough, she now owned.

And to the left of the chair, was Sybil who was seated in a wheelchair. She had grown older but had gotten more beautiful. Her hair was pinned up in a luscious bun, dressed in Swarovski crystals, and she was wearing a designer muumuu speckled with glitter.

But it was the wireless treadmill directly in front of them, that took Nancy's breath away.

"Sit down." The man who brought her inside instructed.

"I don't see an available chair," she said in a shaky voice.

"On the floor." He pointed at his feet.

Slowly the sixty-eight-year-old woman flopped on the floor, causing a shooting pain to run up her spine.

Within thirty minutes the door opened, and Mercy walked inside. Wearing a black velvet tracksuit with a gold cross dangling from her neck, she was both the most beautiful and evil person Nancy had ever seen in her life. Since she had been jogging a towel hung over her shoulder and her natural black hair ran down her back in a ponytail, and her eyes were covered by smokey shades.

What also caught Nancy off guard was her walk, which was both a mixture of femininity and masculinity, and Nancy wondered how easily she played with genders.

Sitting in her king seat, her boyfriend, Black Palmer, kissed her lips and brought her over water and a chalkboard.

She shoved the board away, pulled out her phone and texted: **LEAVE. TAKE SYBIL WITH U.**

He looked at the phone and said, "Naw, I wanna stay here."

She texted: **GO. PLEASE.**

Sighing deeply, he pushed Sybil out of the room and directed. Focusing back on Nancy she said, "Do you know, after all of this time, I still enjoy running." She smiled so brightly it blinded. Now that she was wealthy, her skin was clearer, and her teeth were fixed but her heart was ice cold. "It truly is the one thing I can say I honestly got from you. It's the only thing I ever got from you. That, and, well, knowing how to hold a grudge."

Every one of her men, was in awe. For you see, she still only used her voice, if she intended the person she was talking to directly, to die.

ASK THE STREETS FOR MERCY   165

"Rasha, I —."

Silver Tipped Dreads kicked Nancy in the side, forcing her to cough out blood.

"Mercy." She smiled. "Call me Mercy. You won't be told again."

Nancy wiped the blood from her mouth with the back of her hand. "M...Mercy. I'm sorry."

"Good, so how have you been?"

"My life has been...bad."

She took a sip of water. "I know. I did everything in my power to make it that way."

Her eyes widened. "So, you, you killed my husband?"

"I killed all three." She laughed. "After Mr. Hern died, because you put peanuts in his meal, I noticed you seemed to have a fetish for men who treat you like shit and cheat on you." She took a sip. "So, a bitch here, a poison there, and before long they all were murdered."

"I didn't kill Joe."

"Yes, you did, whore! And you did it because he loved me. Didn't you?"

Nancy rolled over on her knees and threw up. "Why do you still hate me? You, you have ruined my life."

"If you build a monster it's always yours." She held out the water bottle. "Now get on the treadmill."

"Mercy, I—."

"I don't repeat myself."

Slowly Nancy stood up and stepped on the treadmill. At that moment, Mercy was handed a remote control by an Oxford. "If you fall, you die." She hit the button and at first the treadmill started off slow.

And then it went faster.

And then faster.

And faster.

Within two minutes she was barely holding on for life. "Ask for Mercy," she said.

"Mercy!" Nancy cried out without thinking twice. "Please, Mercy! Mercy!"

Instead of slowing down, Mercy clicked the button again. And in the end, she ran so fast she fell off and slammed onto the marble floors. Slowly Mercy rose and stood over her body.

Crying on the floor she said, "Why didn't you just kill me? Why do all of this?"

"Death is easy. But revenge is a sweet long game." With those last words, she was handed a baseball bat that she used to beat her until she didn't have a face. When she was done, she handed it to an Oxford who instructed the others to get rid of the body and clean up the blood.

Her face and cross splattered in blood, she walked to the dining room where Black Palmer sat with Sybil.

"It's over now right?" He asked walking up to her, stroking her shoulders. "You got Nancy so it's over right?"

She grabbed her phone out of her pocket: **HOW IS YOUR COUSIN?**

"Mercy, why aren't you answering my question? Is it over now that you've gotten the one person responsible for it all?"

She wiped the blood out of her face and kissed his lips. Nodding yes, she walked toward Sybil and pushed her toward her room.

When she turned back once, his head was low. She could tell he was growing weary of her need to get revenge. She just hoped he wouldn't leave her until everything was done.

After taking a shower, she tended to Sybil. Every night since she got cancer, she cleaned her up and got her ready for bed. When it came to Black Palmer, who was older than her by eleven years, and Sybil, she would give her full heart.

After she cleaned her and tucked her in bed, Mercy sat on the edge of her mattress. Using her chalkboard, she wrote, HOW DO YOU FEEL

168   *BY T. STYLES*

"Mercy, where is Helena?"

Mercy glared and wrote: WORRY ABOUT YOUR SELF.

She sighed. "How much longer are you going to do these things? Before I die, I want to see you at peace. I want you to let all of this go. Tonight you got the woman responsible for it all. Isn't it time to —"

She waved her hand and angrily wrote: YOU WILL NEVER DIE!

Sybil placed her hand on the chalkboard. "Mercy, I'm sick. Have been this way for quite some time and you know this already. And that's okay. But you can stop all of this. There's still time to turn things around. But not much."

BALTIMORE COUNTY - MALE HOLDING CELL

Farmer was standing in the cell, drawing on the light blue wall, using the corner of a penny he managed to sneak inside. The work was not developed enough to showcase his art, as it was in the beginning stage, but he was focused. Every time he heard a noise in the background he would stop and look around to see who was coming.

He was back to drawing on the walls when a man named Cagney walked inside and gave his thin frame a once over. Flopping on the seat he said, "Fuck is you doing?" He was a big dude with pockmark skin, who took up plenty space.

Farmer scratched his short bushy afro and continued with his work. "As far as I can see, I'm minding my own business."

"Don't get smart, dummy." He slammed his beefy back against the wall. "Because it can be whatever it needs to be up in this bitch."

"Well can it be that you leave me the fuck alone?"

Cagney laughed. "I would get stuck in here with a weirdo."

"My girl don't seem to mind."

He looked at him and shook his head. "No way on earth you got a bitch. So you can go 'head with that shit."

"I do. And she's Asian too." He continued to draw. "Anyway, I only became a weirdo when you walked inside. Prior to that I was doing fine." He scratched at the walls more.

Although Farmer was a brief distraction, Cagney continued to look out of the cell, as his heart thumped wildly in his chest. He was on edge not only because he was snatched off the streets by the police for "questioning", but also because he always got the impression that someone was following him. That someone was watching him.

He just didn't know why.

Cagney was just about to try and get some sleep while praying the police wouldn't hold him for the full 48 when he smelled a foul odor. "Hold up, I know you not over there farting and shit, nigga."

"I'm not about to hold my gas for —."

Unfortunately, he would have to hold his words instead because Cagney leaped on him with the rage of a million men. Knocking him to the floor, the two went at it full force until the bars opened and Greg walked inside with one guard. The years had taken a toll on his face and as a result his light brown skin was greyed and somewhat wrinkled.

When the cell door closed Greg looked at the guard and said, "Hold up, you not gonna break these niggas up first?"

"I ain't in the mood." The guard locked the bars and walked away.

Greg rushed up to the fighting men and with a little effort, pulled them apart. He hated that they were damp and sweaty and already tired. Once separated, Farmer remained near the wall he was posted by while Cagney flopped back on the seat.

"Fuck is going on?" Greg asked out of breath, bent over, the palms of his hand pressed against his knees.

"I was minding my business!" Farmer huffed. "That's what's going on. And this nigga gonna rush me when I had my back turned like a bitch."

Cagney wiped the sweat from his brow. "If farting in a cell full of niggas is minding your business then we gonna have a problem. Because I'm not about to spend whatever time I have in here while you—"

"Okay, okay, everybody calm down," Greg said with extended palms in their direction. "I had a long day and I don't feel like this shit right now." He looked out of the cell, as if his nerves were on edge.

"I don't feel like it either." Farmer said.

"Well prove it and stop the dumb shit." Greg sat on the opposite end of Cagney and ran his hand down his face. Looking over at him he said, "What ya'll in for anyway?"

"This ain't no sharing circle, nigga!"

"We ain't got nothing but time," Greg shrugged. "Might as well talk. I don't know when ya'll got here but they keeping niggas for the full 48-hour hold. I heard that on the way coming in." He looked around from where he sat for cameras.

"I don't know about him, but I prefer not to talk." Farmer continued to draw.

"Whatever, nigga," Greg shrugged. "Makes no difference to me."

BALTIMORE COUNTY - FEMALE HOLDING CELL

Sable was sitting in her cell alone. She was a pretty girl with skin the color of melted honey, but she walked with a slight bop in her step. Her personality fell in between dominate and feminine, but she chose not to subscribe to labels.

She was livid.

Her day started out fucked up and ended up worse. With most of the trouble being brought on herself. She was known for fighting people anytime her temper got the best of her. To some she was a woman who people needed to stay away from. But to Sable, there was a deeper reason she felt the need to fight. After coming out as lesbian a year ago, she wondered if her family or friends would treat her the same. Most didn't, and so she felt alone.

Walking up to the jail cell door she grabbed the bars and looked up and down the hallway. She didn't see anyone, not even a guard, but it didn't mean they weren't watching her from the cameras.

Turning around to look at the one lens pointing her way she yelled, "Why ya'll got me in here? I need to use the phone! Please! Let me out!"

Zeno had been pacing the hallway outside of Labor and Delivery for an hour. He should've been inside holding his baby mother's hand but seeing her in intense pain made him uncomfortable. To look at his build, you'd wonder why such a large man would be so squeamish. After all, Zeno belonged to the streets and had done things most people couldn't imagine.

BY T. STYLES

The years had been hard on him and yet there *still* was a level of regality that transfixed itself on what some would deem to be an ugly face. Tall in stature, he was a gigantic man who owned any room he entered. And women, despite his looks being far from classical, still found him very attractive.

"Oh my, God!" She screamed inside the labor room. "Zeno! Come back in here! Please!"

He didn't want to answer her call, but at the same time it was his duty. Besides, he was the one who had gotten her pregnant. And he would have to muscle up and be at her side.

Taking a deep breath, he pushed back inside the room and looked her way. Her brown face expressed the pain ripping between her legs and she looked exhausted and scared all at once.

"I'm right here, Jono." He stood at her bedside and held her hand. "I'm here." He wiped the moist hair out of her face to see her eyes.

"You're doing good." A nurse coached. "The baby's head is crowning. It'll be just a matter of time now."

"Ahhhh!" She screamed out while pushing at the same time. "It…it hurts!"

As he continued to be there for the birth of his second child, suddenly he glanced up at the door. And what he saw rattled the beast within. Through the small rectangle window, he spotted several officers peering inside at him. By the way they focused on his eyes, he was certain they were there to alter his life.

Maybe forever.

He had done many things, so, he wasn't sure about their purpose. But if they wanted him to go calmly, they would have to wait until his baby was born.

"Just...just push," he said looking at them suspiciously as he directed Jono. "You got this, baby."

"He's almost here!" The midwife yelled from between her legs. "It's just a matter of time! Don't stop pushing."

Just as she gave more instructions, and Jono pushed once more, the baby came sliding out into the world. Right before he could hold his son, the officers came barreling into the room.

"Mr. Bezeno Wright, you're wanted for questioning." They grabbed him on the right and left, with tight firm grips. Destroying the moment and joy of what childbirth represented.

"Questioning for what?" He tried to fight them off, but they maintained their grip. "Let me hold my son!"

"Later for all that!" One of the officers yelled.

Within seconds, he was forcefully taken out of the room. "Fuck is going on? At least tell me that!"

As he was being hauled out by the police, things took a dark turn. *"He's not breathing,"* he heard someone say as he was ushered down the hallway. *"We have to move quick! He's not breathing!"*

Hearing that his son wasn't taking his first breath, sent him on a whirlwind of rage filled emotions. He kicked, moved his head rapidly and tried to get away from the officers.

But it would do him no good.

His son was dead.

CHAPTER 8

BALTIMORE COUNTY – MALE HOLDING CELL

Greg could feel that Farmer and Cagney were about to fight again but he didn't have time for him. The oddest part was, for some reason, they seemed familiar even though he was certain he never met them before. If he had to guess, he thought they were between eighteen and twenty years of age. "I see ya'll young niggas five seconds from tearing off each other's heads. I just want you to know I'm not breaking it up this time."

"I'm not asking for no security guard." Cagney said.

Farmer stopped scratching at the walls and turned around to face him. "Me either. I think we should all stay out of each other's way."

As Greg looked at them, he thought about the days leading up to his arrest.

Mercy

GREG'S STORY

BY T. STYLES

Greg and his seven-year-old son Ocean were walking out of the school. He had been in town only for two years, and his son had gone downhill ever since. The little boy's pace was quick, and Greg didn't know what was happening. Lately he had been annoyed after leaving school and today didn't seem different. Since he was special needs, Greg realized that he had to be smart to find out what was wrong, otherwise he would send him off on an emotional tangent which would inevitably make things worse.

"How was school, son?" He ruffled his curly hair playfully. Something he always did when he first saw him.

"Fine, papa."

He nodded. "Okay, what did you do?"

"We painted."

"All day?"

"Yes, sir."

"Well it sounds to me that you had a really good one." They walked around a little boy and his mother who were looking through his bookbag for his homework. "Because when I was in school, I wished we could play instead of working."

In a low voice he said, "Not me."

Now he was concerned, but somewhat proud. "You like to do your work more than play?"

"Yes, sir. I wish, I wish, I could be left alone."

He frowned. "Ocean, I want to ask you something, but I don't want you to get upset. Because you know how things are when you get upset don't you?"

"Yes, sir, my head hurts."

He smiled. "Right, and I don't want your head hurting okay?"

"Yes, sir." He nodded softly.

He stopped walking and grabbed his little hand. "Okay, tell me what's wrong with —."

Suddenly Ocean went ballistic and started pounding at his face and head with his free hand. The rant was loud and awkward, and he was growing attention from all those who were near. So, he began singing to him instead. Something he'd done in the past to calm his nerves.

"You're the best little boy in…"

Not listening, Ocean continued to hit himself more, so hard that he doubted he'd be able to hear anything he was singing. Looking around he said, "Ocean, stop hurting yourself, son. Please."

When he didn't stop, he picked him up and placed his lips closely against his ear and sang softer. *"You're* the best little boy in the whole wide world. *The whole wide world. The whole wide world. You're the best little boy in the whole wide world and I love you so much."*

It took some time, but after a while, Ocean calmed down and wrapped his arms around his father's neck in a firm hug. It was the best feeling. To say the man loved his son was an understatement.

"Ready to go home?"

He sniffled and wiped his tears away. "Yes, sir. I think so."

It took some time, but two hours later, Greg had gotten little Ocean ready for the birthday party he was invited to earlier in the week. Since the house was only two blocks down, they decided to walk instead of drive.

"How you doing?" He asked looking down at him. He seemed calm in the moment, but he couldn't be sure. He just wished he knew what was troubling his kid all of a sudden. "Are you ready to have fun?"

"Yes, sir." He grinned proudly and raised the small blue and white gift box in his hand that he brought for his friend. "You think he will like it?"

"I know he will, son." He grinned. "You picked a good one."

Ocean smiled proudly which made Greg's heart melt. It was hard being a single father, but he did so with graciousness and love. He would do it all over again if he had to because he meant so much to him. Ocean taught him patience. Ocean taught him strength. But more than anything, Ocean taught him love. And that was a tough chore because growing up, he was a very selfish man who hurt women for fun.

They were almost at the house which was holding the party when suddenly they saw guests giving them strange looks as they entered. Greg, sensing something was off, stopped walking.

"What's wrong, papa?" Ocean asked looking up to him.

"I don't know."

He wanted to ask his son what happened at school earlier, because he was certain by the looks, that something had occurred to warrant such dark stares.

Greg stopped walking. "Ocean, I don't know if we should go to the party today, son." The last thing he needed was his boy getting his feelings hurt again, which would cause him to go ballistic.

"But whyyyyyy?"

"Because..." Before he could finish, the mother of the student throwing the party walked out of her house and up to them.

"Hello, Greg." She crossed her arms tightly over her body. So tightly he thought she would cut herself in half.

He nodded. "Is everything okay, Amanda?"

"Yes," she looked down at Ocean and smiled. "He looks cute with his little bowtie and all."

"What's up, Amanda?" Greg said shifting a little. He didn't feel like the games or the short talk.

She dropped her hands down. "Well, unfortunately, we won't be allowing Ocean to come to the house today."

"Why the fuck not?" He shrugged. "He got an invitation."

The fake smile she wore on her face melted and in its place was a sinister glare. "Ask your child. He knows." She stomped away.

Greg looked down. "Ocean, what happened in class?"

He began to tremble. "I'm not supposed to tell."

He lowered his height and got on his knees. He didn't care that everyone was still watching them. Taking a deep breath and looking into his eyes he asked, "Ocean, son, tell me what happened in school today."

"I cut their hair."

He frowned. "Whose hair?"

"All the little girls."

"Why?"

Silence.

He grabbed his hand. "Ocean, why did you do that?"

"Because she told me to."

"Who is she?"

"I'm not supposed to tell." He cried.

CHAPTER 9

BALTIMORE COUNTY - FEMALE HOLDING CELL

Sable sat in her cell, irritated that no one bothered to give her more information on what she was going to be questioned about. It was getting annoying because not only did she hate being in jail, but when she looked down on the seat she was sitting on, she realized she just came on her period.

"Fuck, fuck, fuck," she said to herself, as she looked at her fingertips after touching herself between her legs. "Not now." She whispered. "Not fucking now."

With the back of her pants covered in blood, she approached the bars again. "I need help!"

"Shut up!" A guard yelled. "You been screaming all day and I'm sick of your mouth."

"If you fucking helped me you wouldn't have to worry about hearing my mouth!" She gripped the bars tighter.

The guard approached the cell. "If you keep fucking with me, I'ma give you a reason to yell." He stroked his dick. "Now shut the fuck up and wait until the investigators call your name."

Slowly she backed up and flopped in her seat. As her mind remembered what she was doing before she was arrested.

SABLE'S STORY

Sable sat on the floor with her back against the wall inside of her bedroom within her apartment in Baltimore City. She was holding a brown leather book, which was tattered around the edges. When she pulled open the yellowing pages, that were once white, she took a deep breath and read the first line.

Of all things I am sorry for, the most thing that brings me pain, is having a gay daughter. I can deal with anything else, and I do. But if she was never born, it would have made me a very happy man.

"Sable…"

She jumped when she heard the voice and closed the diary. But when she looked up and saw the tall light skin girl with long brown hair reaching down her back she smiled. "Hunter."

"You left the door opened." She said in a soft voice.

"I know. I told you I would."

"Then why you seem shocked when I called your name?"

"Have you ever felt like somebody was hunting you down? Even though there's no reason for you to feel that way?"

She shook her head. "No. Because I'm living right."

"I'm serious." She sighed. "Ever since I can remember, it always felt as if somebody was out to get me."

"You deserve peace."

She looked at her with lustful eyes. "What I deserve is some pussy. You gonna give it to me or not. I left the door unlocked not so you can lecture me. But so you would put out. So, the question is, are you fucking me or what? We don't have a lot of time."

"You always get your way." She removed her shirt and tossed it to the floor. "And you love taking risks too don't you?"

"I do." She nodded.

"That's gonna get you killed one day."

"Then at least I'll die having fun."

Hunter dropped her skirt and then her panties. Stepping out of the pile, she walked over to Sable and removed her pants followed by her boxers. Shoving her back on the bed she said, "Who said it would be fun?"

After a minute of banter, they were just about to get it in when Ebony, Sable's girlfriend walked into their bedroom. Her heart dropped. Quickly she shoved Hunter off of her body and she made a thud against the floor.

Grabbing her shorts, Sable got to the business of copping a plea. All of this was a shock, because as far as she knew, her girl had to work tonight. So, what was she doing home?

"What...what's going on?" Ebony asked looking at the women with a rotating stare.

"Baby, I was just...I was just—."

"Don't!" She yelled pointing at her. "You don't get to tell me you were playing. You don't get to fuck another bitch in my bed either!" She wiped her eyes. "You proved who you are, and I will never forgive you for this."

Sable ran behind her, but she slammed the door in her face. "Fuck!"

CHAPTER 10

Zeno sat in the back of the cruiser, still trying to understand what he was being questioned about. It was as if the police were breaking every law, and not giving a fuck about it either. It was messing up his mind that one minute he was about to watch the birth of his son, and the next minute he was in the back of a squad car.

"...so, I don't know what to get her," Officer Charles said as he escorted him in his cruiser as he sat behind a thick stained plastic wall. "I mean she claims she doesn't want to know the sex of the baby, but I think she does." He chuckled. "Women are that way you know?" He looked back at Zeno. "Picky and not being able to make up their minds. Drives me wild."

Zeno looked toward the window.

Why the man was intent on pulling him into his life was beyond him. Didn't he understand the pain he was in at the moment? Didn't he realize the turmoil he felt, not knowing if his son survived?

"And there's a reason I want to make the first gift special." Officer Charles continued basically talking to himself. "Well, I kinda got her sister pregnant."

Zeno looked at him and shook his head.

He didn't care.

"Don't judge me." He said eyeing him through the rearview mirror. "We all the same way. I'm talking about men. So that means you too."

"I guess." He said under his breath.

"I would think with you being a brother and all, you would understand where I'm coming from."

"Fuck that supposed to mean?"

"Well it's common knowledge that black men aren't able to be monogamous."

"Ain't you black?"

"Yeah, but, well, I'm actually mixed." The officer continued, turning left. "So, it makes me a bit different."

He chuckled. "My man, you still a nigga." He paused. "Get caught on the wrong road one night out of that uni and you'll see."

Officer Charles' face reddened. Zeno hit a nerve and for some reason he loved that he was rattled. Normally he wasn't the type to antagonize. But the callousness in which the officer handled what he was going through at the moment rubbed him the wrong way.

"Like I was saying," the officer continued. "I was thinking I have a good idea on what to buy, since I owe her and all for stepping out the relationship. After all, it's not her fault her sister has a badder body. My girl was pregnant before, so her frame fell differently with this baby. She gonna need surgery to put everything back in place."

Zeno shook his head.

"Anyway, I was thinking, instead of getting her a gift for the baby, I would buy her a treadmill. It's my way of saying I won't cheat on her again, if she keeps shit right. Now I can't say if it's true or not. Seeing as how her sister's pussy is wetter and I may fuck her again, but at least it'll make her feel better. Because right now she's—."

"My man, I don't give a fuck."

Officer Charles slowed down. "What you just say to me?"

"I said I don't give a fuck about all that noise you talking. And unless you gonna tell me what the fuck I'm being questioned for, I would appreciate you leaving me the fuck alone."

The officer sped up a little, although he was still going much slower than what was necessary to get to the precinct in reasonable time. Before long, they were passing tall trees on a dark road.

The travel plans had changed that's for sure.

"Where we going?" Zeno asked looking around the car.

Silence.

"Where you taking me?" Zeno said a bit louder.

The officer looked at him through the rearview mirror and continued to drive without saying a word.

When they were further and further away from the precinct the officer stopped on a treelined street, with no people or houses in eyesight. Taking a deep breath, he turned off the car. It was completely dark in the vehicle.

Zeno's heart pumped within his chest, because with his hands cuffed behind his back, he was definitely at the officer's mercy. "You should be careful."

Zeno sat back. "Meaning?"

"You should know when to show a little respect. And if you feel you can't, you should know when to fake it. It could mean the difference between life and death."

"My nigga, what you gonna do? Because the way I feel, I don't give a fuck no more."

Officer Charles sat in the dark car with him for five more minutes, before turning the engine back on and pulling off.

BALTIMORE COUNTY - MALE HOLDING CELL

Despite many threats from Cagney, Farmer was sitting on the toilet relieving himself. Every time he shit, he courtesy flushed but the cell was still funky, and this made Cagney livid.

Although they were angry, his mind went back to the hours leading up to his arrest.

FARMER'S STORY

Farmer stood behind his friend Bart who was in a liquor store. His friend just cashed his check and he was in a good mood. Tapping Farmer on the back he said, "Thanks for rolling with me. What you about to do now?"

Since Farmer was broke, he shrugged. "Nothing, I guess."

"Nah, I'm taking you out for drinks." He slapped him on the shoulder again, which was his favorite thing to do.

An hour later they were in the bar on their second drink. Bart was a loud bastard when he was drunk, and the tolerable side to his personality went out the window. Leaving behind a monster.

"So when you gonna dump that stupid bitch?"

He glared. "What you talking about?"

"I know you can't be serious about sticking with that whore." He laughed, slamming his beer on the counter. "She takes the little money you make, treats you like shit and —."

"What happens between me and my girl is my business."

Bart looked at him for a moment and broke out into laughter. "Okay, well is it also your business when you beg me to come pick you up after she throws you out? Or is it your business when you ask to borrow money because you ain't making enough tips at the restaurant? Or —."

"You talk a lot of shit." Farmer said cutting him off. "Someday somebody gonna make you swallow it, so you can see how it tastes."

Bart paused for a moment and laughed harder. "Well who that gonna be? You?" He pointed a stiff finger into his chest. "Because we both know you can't handle me if you tried."

Farmer looked down. The rage he was feeling was unprecedented and suddenly his stomach started churning.

Bart slapped him on the back violently hard. "Now let's quit all this fighting." He grabbed his wallet that was pulsating with cash. "As long as I got money, you'll never be broke." He waved the bartender over.

"Yes, sir." The bartender said wiping the counter.

"Bring us another round. And don't worry about giving my man the check. He ain't got no money." He looked at him and winked. "But I got him."

The bartender nodded and walked away.

When he started texting on his phone, Farmer reached into his pocket and removed his gun. With it gripped in his palm, he was about to stick it into his waist to rob him for what was left of his paycheck, which was always the plan, until he felt a hand on his shoulder.

Quickly he stuffed the weapon back. "What you doing here, Stacey?" He asked looking around, before looking back at her. She was a pretty girl with winged eye makeup and a large smile.

"Yeah, what the fuck you doing here?" Bart asked standing over Farmer's shoulder.

To stop a fight, since he knew Bart didn't like her, Farmer escorted her outside. "What's going on, Stacey? Why you here?"

"Because I don't want you to do what you're about to do."

He looked behind him and walked a bit further from the bar. "But you told me to do it. Said you were tired of me being broke and—."

"I know but I was wrong."

He wiped his hand down his face. To think that he was five seconds from robbing his friend only to hear her say never mind, fucked with him. "What made you change? One minute you were—."

"I told you already."

He looked down the street, at the bar and back into her eyes. "I just want you to know that I would do anything for you. I never thought I would be able to date a half black and half Asian girl and—."

"So that's the only reason you got with me? Because you think I'm exotic?"

"No, I mean, I just like having you on my arm that's all."

"Good, because we have to talk about a few more things. And I don't know if you'll like what I'm about to say."

CHAPTER 11

When Zeno walked through the precinct with Officer Charles to go through intake, every prisoner and officer looked in awe upon his huge frame. He had the type of build that had to cooperate in order to be taken into custody, unless you had more than one man to handle him if he got out of hand. Luckily for all those present, at the moment anyway, he was willing.

After an hour, he was processed and taken to a cell that had a phone inside. He had been in jail before and knew most of the time the phones didn't work. So, it was best waiting until he heard the dial tone before growing too excited.

When he lifted the headset, the dial tone sang in his ear.

Zeno took a deep breath and called everyone he could think of, but no one answered. He was concerned about his girl. He was concerned about their baby. And he was concerned about his family. Without anyone picking up, he was left with more questions than answers, and that alone drove him mad.

After calling his mother two more times, finally she answered. Relieved to hear her voice, he slammed a fist into the cream tiled wall. "Ma, why you ain't pick up when I hit you a second ago?"

There was loud music playing, and she turned it down. "Because I was bringing the groceries in the house. Where are you anyway?"

"In jail."

"Bezeno, not again!"

"It's not what you think it is." He ran a hand down his face. "At least I don't think so. But you gotta listen." He looked behind him to make sure no one was ear hustling. "I think, I think something is wrong with my girl."

"What do you mean something is wrong? I'm preparing the food for the birth of my grandson. So, I'm expecting a baby on this end. Didn't you take her to the hospital? She was dilated when she—."

"Ma, the baby, I think, I'm not sure if he made it."

Silence.

"Ma."

She sighed. "Bezeno, I hope your baby is alive because I want to meet my grandson. And I would like to tell you I'm surprised if something did go wrong but I'm not."

He frowned. "Ma, now is not the time to—."

"Not the time to what?" She interrupted. "Tell you like it is? To be honest with my boy? Because if anytime is not a perfect time to talk real to you, I don't know what else to say."

He grinded his teeth. "I'm listening."

"Good. Because this story won't be long. At the end of the day, I don't trust the girl. Never have and never will."

"So, it's Juno's fault that she lost our baby?"

"Could be."

"Ma."

"I caught her taking something orally a few months ago. When I asked what it was, she didn't seem to have an answer."

"Well what you think it was?" He shuffled around a little. "I'm in jail right now and I don't have time for—."

"It was liquid. In a bottle. She said it was prenatal vitamins, but I've raised ten children, two of my own, and have given you all every vitamin known to man. And I never saw what was in that bottle before in my life." She sighed. "Now I pray my grandson is okay. But with her as the mother, son, I can't be sure."

Silence.

"Bezeno, are you there?"

His jaw twitched. "Yeah."

"I know this is the last thing you wanted to hear from your mother. And I hate that I had to bring this to you. But I have a feeling that she never wanted to have a baby. I have a feeling the purpose was to hurt you, because we all know you wanted a son. Something else is up with that girl. Trust me."

"I gotta go."

"What about your bail?"

"I'll hit you if I need you to go to the stash. But I'ma work it out."

"I love you, son."

"Later, ma."

His relationship with his girlfriend was different. It was true. She appeared to come out of nowhere when she entered his life a few years earlier. With everything going on, it was at a time when he needed someone. She didn't care that he could never submit his whole heart. She didn't care that he would forever be in love with another. She wanted to be his protector. And considering he was all man; those were big shoes to fill.

She did a good job in the beginning.

In fact, without her over the past few years, the streets would've had his body, blood and soul because he was reckless. But when she came into the picture, those things were off limits.

He just hoped she wasn't a scam.

BALTIMORE COUNTY - MALE HOLDING CELL

Cagney had left the cell earlier in the evening. Greg and Farmer believed it was to make a phone call since their cell didn't have one, but they couldn't be sure. Farmer was still drawing on the wall, while Greg was posted up on the bench worried above all.

"I heard you talking to Cagney about your son earlier." Farmer said. "And him not being able to go to the party. Was that the reason you got arrested?"

Greg sighed.

Farmer looked over at him. "Just say you don't wanna talk."

"It ain't that I don't want to talk. I'm just irritated. I haven't gotten my phone call and I don't know what's going on." He looked toward the cell door. "I think these niggas playing games with my life. What I don't know is why?"

While still drawing he said, "Well tell me what you were doing before you got arrested. And maybe I'll tell you too."

GREG'S STORY

Greg popped up in bed and when he realized he was late getting his son ready for school; his anxiety levels rose. Although he loved spending time with his son, he truly needed the break while he was at school. It was often hard for people to remember that Ocean was special needs because he looked normal. In fact, he was downright adorable. But that didn't mean he wasn't a handful and almost difficult to manage.

Losing time, quickly he went about getting everything ready. He picked out his outfit. Stuffed his son's backpack with his crayons and papers. And even made his lunch. When he was done, he went to his son's room to wake him up, which was always easier said than done. "Get up, Ocean. We running late."

He moaned a little but didn't rise.

"Son, you have to get up and go to school." He nudged him a bit harder. "Stop playing now."

He pulled the covers over his head. "I don't wanna go."

Greg sat on the edge of the bed. "Why? You used to love school."

He pulled the sheet down. "Not anymore."

"Ocean, who was the person who told you to cut those little girls' hair? Because you were suspended for five days and I don't want you having the same problem today."

"I can't say."

"Well was it a kid?"

He stared at him and suddenly Ocean started slapping at his own head. Not wanting him to have a big breakdown before school, Greg gripped him tightly and held him in his arms until he calmed down.

It took some time, but an hour later, they were walking to his school. Normally the trip before class would make his behavior a bit better. Because he would be somewhat tired. But today he still appeared tense.

Right before they reached the door, Ocean took off running in the opposite direction. He was so quick, that Greg couldn't find him within the thickness of the students. After some time, Greg's nerves were so bad

BY T. STYLES

trying to locate his boy that he doubled back. He wanted to know which little girl had frightened his boy so much, that he was afraid to enter the building.

Suddenly he started snatching little girls by the arms left and right. Anyone who he deemed had a messy face, without caring about how they felt, he would yank them up by the wrists.

"What you know about what's going on with my boy?" He asked one.

"Ouch, you're hurting me!" She yelled, while trying to get away.

"Do you know Ocean or not?"

He continued to question kids, hoping that one of them would tell him what had been troubling his son. In the end, he yanked up eight little girls and was on his way to a ninth when a teacher and school officer came running outside. He was definitely giving up creep pedophile vibes.

Greg, realizing he had gone too far, took off running.

An hour later, he was home with no answers. He had called the police and filed a report because he was worried sick. Looking for clues, he decided to go through Ocean's bookbag. It was then that he found a piece of paper with the words ASK THE STREETS FOR MERCY written on it in crayon. That note sent chills down his spine. He always knew it was a mistake to return home. But he figured after fifteen years, his past would not catch up with him.

He thought wrong.

When there was a knock at the door, he yanked it open. There were five officers waiting on the other side. "Please tell me you have my son." He said.

Instead of answering his question, they took him away in cuffs.

BALTIMORE COUNTY - MALE HOLDING CELL

Cagney and Farmer sat across from each other looking at Greg as he told his story.

"So, hold up, you got arrested for grabbing up kids?" Farmer asked.

"I don't know why they took me," he shook his head. "They said they wanted me for questioning. So that's the only thing I can think of that went wrong."

Farmer started drawing again. "Sounds strange."

Greg grew annoyed. "What you trying to say?"

"Nothing, but it sounds like they got you for messing with kids."

"First of all, you ain't gotta believe me." He paused. "I ain't fucking with no kids. But something is definitely going on with my son. And as messed up as things have been going in my life, for some reason I feel like they're connected." He got up and walked toward the bars. "And I still don't know where my son is. But they better tell me something. Because I'm about to blow."

CHAPTER 12

INTERROGATION ROOM

Sable was taken to an interrogation room by a guard. When she walked inside the small room, two officers were waiting. Both wearing button down white shirts with black leather gun holsters. If they weren't different races they'd look like twins.

"Have a seat," Officer Watkins said. He was a black man in his fifties with a soft grey bush. His partner, Miriam, was the exact opposite. A white man in his early forties with blonde hair. And both seemed to be disgusted with her at the moment.

She took her seat and for some reason began rubbing the table with flat palms. "Can somebody tell me what's going on?"

"What do you think is going on?" Officer Miriam said scratching his blond beard. "We want to hear from you."

"From me?" She chuckled and sat back. "I don't know. But I do know I'm funky. I'm tired and I wanna go home." She sighed. "So, tell me something."

"You're a very attractive girl," Watkins said. "But I don't have to tell you that. I'm sure you already know."

She shrugged her right shoulder. "I do alright I guess."

"Who's Johanna Howard?"

Sable's mouth opened and closed.

"Sable...who is she?" Miriam asked.

"I...I don't know."

The officers looked at one another. "So, you want us to believe you don't know who she is when the look on your face says something totally different?"

"Who is she?" Watkins persisted. "And do yourself a favor and hold the fucking lies."

SABLE'S STORY

It was raining hard and Sable was bored at home. To put it frankly, life for her had dragged since she and her girlfriend decided to live a domestic lifestyle a year ago. And as a result, she longed for excitement. She longed for the spark she thought would get her blood going.

She longed for drama.

Even after her girl took her back after catching her with Hunter in their room, preparing to fuck, still Sable wanted trouble. To be honest Sable would have preferred Ebony go off and fight her for the incident, but that's not what happened, and she wondered why.

Lying back to back with her girl who was fast asleep, she turned her head to verify her slumber. When she was certain she was gone to the world, she grabbed her cell phone off the side table. When she did, she realized she had several notifications from a beautiful woman.

Despite her beauty, the first thing she noticed about the girl was her personality. Her current woman was older and had a tendency to bore her into submission, but this girl had the same dry humor she did. Based on her profile, she appeared to find dark things funny and for some reason, it drew her in even more.

Tiring of speaking to her via text, when the girl made an offer to meet her that night, she crept out of bed, jumped into the spare clothing she kept in the hallway and hopped into her car. Within the hour she was at the Marking Nightclub.

Just the excitement of getting caught did something to Sable's spirit, and she couldn't wait to see if she was as bold as she put on when they were texting. Did she really want them to fuck in the bathroom? Or was it all a game? Sable wanted her to back up every word.

Feeling like a kid in the candy store, Sable was staring around the busy nightclub, looking for the girl with the red tights and white t-shirt. Suddenly someone's hands hung heavily on her shoulders from behind and Sable smiled.

"You're on time I see." Sable said.

She walked in front of her and extended her hand. "I'm Johanna Howard. It's nice to meet you." She shook her fingers and it was soft and dainty. And every time she spoke, her long black hair hung over the cut-up t-shirt she wore that revealed her cleavage.

"I know who you are."

Johanna smiled and it lit up the room. "So, what you want to do?"

"Naw," Sable said waving the air. "You talked big shit and now I'm here. I need you to back up everything you said on the phone."

"I'm gonna do that and more." She nodded slowly. "Don't worry." She sighed. "But first I have a question. Why do you cheat? On your girl?"

The smile on Sable's face wiped away. "What you talking about?"

"I asked you a specific question. If your life is so good, why do you cheat?"

"Why does anybody do anything?" She shrugged.

"Why do you want to be with a person who cheats? How about that."

She looked down. "Listen, all I want is to have a little fun. To get to know you better. To—."

"You know what...let me stop you." Suddenly the woman with all the questions was creeping her out. After all, Sable was just hemmed up with Hunter. The last thing she needed was for this to go wrong because she told her girl. Perhaps this was all a set up. "Maybe I should bounce."

She turned to walk away, but Johanna gripped her by her wrist and held on tightly. "Naw, I want you to chill here for a little while."

"But—."

"Let's do what we talked about on the phone. And if you don't like how I feel after that, I'll let you go."

Five minutes later they were in the stall. Johanna sat on the back of the bowl; legs wide open while Sable was sitting in front of her, going to work eating her out. When the sensation got too much to handle, she gripped the back of Sable's head and pushed her thick pussy into her lips.

They didn't care that people were walking into the bathroom. It was all about the moment. It was all about the feeling.

But it was also about much more.

THE INTERROGATION ROOM

"So, we are going to ask you again," Miriam said sliding a picture in her direction. "Do you know Johanna or not?"

Sable sat back in her seat. She knew everything was weighing on her answer. And at the same time, she didn't feel like complying. "Like I said, the answer is no, I've never met this person before a day in my life."

"Well I don't believe you." Watkins stood up. "In fact, we know that you have a history of violence against women."

She frowned. "You don't know shit about me."

"On the contrary, young man," Miriam said. "I know everything about you."

Sable's jaw twitched. She could do without being disrespected as a woman. "You know only what you think you—."

"Do you remember Kimmy?" Miriam asked.

She moved a little in her seat. She did know her. Very well.

"Or are you going to lie like you're doing about Johanna?" He continued.

"I know her. She was the..." she cleared her throat. "She was the first girl I was ever with sexually."

"And what did you do to her, when you found out she was using you for your money? And started dating your male best friend instead?"

"I was young."

"You beat her so badly, she was unrecognizable to her friends and family." Watkins said. "That's what you did."

"Like I said, I was young. And we became friends after that."

"There's no such thing as friendship, when fear is the connector." Miriam continued. "That girl stayed cordial with you, until she and her family moved to Florida and never spoke to you again."

Sable looked down. "That's not the whole story."

"Do you know Johanna or not?" Watkins persisted.

She looked up at him. "I said no."

"What about Corrine? The girl you started dating in secret two years ago. No different from Kimmy, she also left you. And how did you repay her?"

Suddenly Sable's head began to throb. "I want to get out of here."

"How did you fucking repay her?" He yelled, slamming a flat palm on the table. "Tell me!"

She shifted a little in her seat. "We had a fight."

"No, you burned her car, with her inside. The girl barely escaped with her life." Watkins paused. "None of the women testified against you. Most were young and too scared. But you won't get away with the murder of Johanna."

Sable's eyes widened. "Wait, Johanna is dead?"

"I thought you didn't know her." Watkins responded.

"I don't...I mean...I did...I mean..."

"Welllll...well, well. Looks like we caught a liar."

CHAPTER 13

BALTIMORE COUNTY - MALE HOLDING CELL

Zeno was escorted into the cell where Greg, Cagney and Farmer waited. The moment Zeno saw Greg, he dragged his hands down his face while Greg looked into the ceiling in annoyance.

"I take it you two know each other," Cagney said.

"Yeah, unfortunately we do." Greg said looking at Zeno. "What you in here for?"

"Does it matter?" Zeno shrugged. "You don't fuck with me, and I don't fuck with you. So, let's leave it at that."

"He can't do it." Cagney said to Zeno.

"Yeah, he likes getting into people's business." Farmer cosigned. "Been doing it all night. Asking questions about who we are and shit."

Zeno had zero time for the noise. In fact, the last time he saw Greg was the night of the party at Kadir and Nalo's house. And after what happened that night, he hoped to never see him again.

"As long as you stay the fuck away from me, I'm good." Zeno said looking squarely into Greg's eyes.

"So, I guess that means you won't tell me what you arrested for." Greg continued sitting down.

Zeno looked at him and shook his head. The truth was he didn't know why he was brought in for questioning. And at the same time, he had an idea.

ZENO'S STORY

Zeno's house in Upper Marlboro, Maryland was filled to capacity.

Considered the Plug to many on the streets, he was known to keep fifteen hitters with him at all times. He was just about to speak to his men about the upcoming package, when Flower, his fifteen-year-old daughter walked into the room. She clearly took after her mother in the looks department because she was so beautiful Zeno's men often looked away, to prevent having lustful thoughts.

When he saw her face, he rose and hugged her, before walking her away from his men. He wasn't one for talking business around his baby girl and he kept to that moral. Standing in his room he said, "What you doing here? I told you I was discussing business tonight."

"I know, dad." She looked at the men through the opened doorway and then back at him. "It's just that, I'm gonna say something and I don't want you to get mad."

He shifted a little. "What is it?" He placed heavy hands on her shoulders.

"I'm pregnant."

He took one step back but then stepped closer. "Pregnant? What you mean you're pregnant?"

"Daddy, I'm sure you know how it happens seeing as though I'm about to have a little brother in a few days. So please don't make me—."

"That's not what I asked you. I never seen you with a nigga. How did this happen?"

"Daddy, we are in love."

His nostrils pulsated. "Flower, who is he?"

"Daddy, you're flaring."

"Who is he?" He said a bit louder causing her to blink repeatedly.

"I don't want to say. Not when you're like this."

"You're fifteen years old."

"I know." She rubbed her belly. "But this is still happening."

BY T. STYLES

He tried to calm down, but the anger was too intense in the moment. "I can't believe this."

"I know, daddy. And I'm so sorry for disappointing you. I just—."

"It's not about disappointing me. I...I..." He couldn't talk at the moment. "Listen, I need to get my mind together. Give me five minutes. Wait out there."

She kissed him on the cheek and said, "Okay." She closed the door behind herself.

As he sat on the edge of the bed in his room, he thought about all the faces of the little niggas who swooned over her when he dropped her off at school. He thought about the crew of fast girls she ran with and vowed to forbid her to hang with them in the future. He didn't have a direct plan to protect her, but he was getting a lot of good ideas.

Most of all, he thought about his failures due to wanting a son so badly.

Because at the end of the day, he dropped the ball with his firstborn. And as a result, his daughter was pregnant.

It was settled, he would have to talk to Flower in the morning. If she was going to have the baby, it would be brought into the world the right way. But first he had to manage his crew.

When he opened the bedroom door to resume his meeting, he saw one of his youngest soldiers, Davon, touching the small of his daughter's back as he whispered in her ear. While the tapes played back in his mind in the moment, he remembered how they always seemed to laugh at each other's jokes. How they always seemed to find themselves sitting next to one another when Zeno hosted a family and friend's dinner.

Why hadn't he seen this before?

It had to be him.

The betrayal made him dizzy.

In a rage, he snatched the boy up by the back of his shirt. Turning him around, he hit him in the center of the nose repeatedly, until it smashed so much, it looked like a glob of red and brown jelly hanging from the center of his face.

Five minutes later, the others managed to get Zeno off of Davon. It wasn't as if they hadn't been trying. It's just that his monstrous strength prevented them from doing so.

When he went to clean himself up in the bathroom, and returned to the living room, Davon had the door open. A white bloodied rag covered the center of his face. And the police were on the other side.

BALTIMORE COUNTY - MALE HOLDING CELL

Zeno thought about beating Davon up yesterday for possibly fucking his daughter.

If he were going to be locked up, he would think that would be the reason. But it turned out the police were there looking for one of his other men, for an open warrant. But when asked about Davon's face by the officers, Davon claimed he had trouble with bloody noses. The police ended up dropping the subject besides, they didn't have proof.

Did Davon go back to the police later and file a report after all?

"I know you don't want to talk about why you in here," Greg said to Zeno as he sat next to him in the cell. "And to be honest, I don't blame you. I let you down."

"You betrayed me." Zeno corrected him. "There's a difference."

Farmer shook his head and continued to scratch at the wall with his penny. "Maybe you should just leave him alone."

"Maybe you should mind your fucking business." Greg responded.

For some reason, Zeno's eyes rested on Cagney. Sitting up straight he said, "Who's your father?"

He scratched his belly. "Why?"

Zeno glared. "Because I asked you."

"And just like you don't feel like talking to my man right here, I don't feel like answering no questions either."

"I'm—."

"Come on, Cagney." One of the guards said approaching the bars. "They're ready for you."

Cagney got up and walked quickly toward the bars. When he left, both Zeno and Greg looked at one another. There was something very familiar about the boy, and Greg felt stupid for not trusting his gut earlier.

"He doesn't look familiar to you?" Zeno asked.

Greg nodded his head slowly. "Yeah…I got a feeling I knew him but couldn't place where from."

INTERROGATION ROOM

Cagney sat across from Miriam and Watkins trembling. He was a big dude, but nothing scared him on the planet more than the police.

"Are you gay?" Watkins asked.

He frowned. "Gay?"

The officers looked at one another. "You want me to say it again?" Watkins responded.

"I heard you the first time. Just confused on why you asking that's all." He shrugged.

"We're trying to get to know you." Miriam said.

"Okay, well are *you* gay?" Cagney smiled at his own humor.

"This is definitely serious." Watkins responded, flipping through the file in front of him.

"Listen, if this is about my traffic tickets, I'm sorry. But other than that, I don't know why ya'll got me hemmed up. I been in a cell all day with a nigga shitting, and another nigga asking a bunch of questions. Tell me something, man."

They looked at one another.

"We going to be straight forward; do you know a woman by the name of Johanna Howard?"

"Jo...uh...um..."

"Do you know her or not?"

He swallowed the lump in his throat. "No, I, I don't know who she is."

They slid a picture across the table. "Are you sure?"

He didn't look.

"Cagney, look at it."

Slowly his eyes rolled down and he focused on the photo. Taking another swallow, he thought about the past.

CAGNEY'S STORY

It was raining outside when Johanna showed up at the tattoo shop. Cagney, who had just finished tattooing ten people that night was exhausted and ready to go home. Still, for some reason, he decided to let trouble inside.

Bad move.

"You can't stay long," he said walking up to his station. "I'm on my way out."

She followed him. "Why would I stay long when we never need much time?"

"I'm serious." He placed his laptop into his bag. "It's been a long day and I don't feel like fucking around tonight."

"So, you don't even have time to get some of this pussy?" She rubbed herself between the legs.

When he turned around, he was shocked to see her standing in the middle of the floor naked from the waist down. The girl moved quickly.

Slowly she pushed him on the chair and eased on top of him. Before he could say a word, she stuffed his stiff dick into her waiting body. She was warm, tight and soft and he loved everything about her juiciness.

As she moved up and down, he couldn't get over how beautiful she was as her hair draped over her face, almost as if she were tickling him. Every time he pumped her curls would brush his cheeks. Loving the sensation, he gripped her hips hard, as he continued to move in and out of her body. Her pussy was all the right things, and so was her face, but he couldn't understand why he didn't like the bitch.

At all.

When they were done, while she remained on top of him, she took a pocketknife from her bra and sliced a mark on her inner arm. Something she had done every time they made love. When she was finished, she licked the knife, folded it and tucked it back into her bra.

Annoyed, he took a deep breath, grabbed her by the waist and pushed her off of him. Immediately. Her bare feet slapped against the cold floor.

"What's wrong?" She asked with a wide grin on her face.

He fastened his pants. "I can't fuck with you no more."

"Fuck you mean you can't fuck with me?"

"Just what I said. I mean you were cool at first, but now you borderline crazy and I can't with this shit. I been told you that."

She grabbed her panties and slipped into her tights. Walking up to him quickly she grabbed his hands. "There's another reason you're doing this. Be a man and tell me what the fuck is up!"

"Okay, it's like this…when I was fucking with you, when we first got together, I was messed up because I just broke up with my lady. She owns this shop. But now, I mean, now it just ain't in me to be with you."

"You could've said something before I marked up my body, Cagney."

He frowned. "I never asked you to do that stupid shit! That's one of the reasons I'm dumping you now! You don't get it."

She stood in front of him for a minute in silence. Finally, she took a deep breath. "Whatever happens to me from here on out is your fault. Remember that." She ran out of the door, leaving him alone.

INTERROGATION ROOM

"We're tired of playing games, Cagney." Miriam said loudly. "You either tell us how you know this girl or risk being locked up for the rest of your life. Your choice."

He looked at the picture and sat back in the chair. "Like I said, I don't know this person. It's as simple as that."

"That's too bad. Because we have reason to believe you do. And since you pretending you don't know her, you should also know that she's dead."

CHAPTER 14
INTERROGATION ROOM

Farmer strutted into the interrogation room holding his lower belly. His irritable bowel syndrome was on one. The plan was to say less and let them talk. Besides, although he just met Greg, he warned him against telling them anything they should already know.

And so, Farmer opened his mouth, preparing to say, *lawyer*, when Miriam said, "I caution you against what you're about to do."

Farmer frowned. "How you know what I'm about to do?"

"Because we know everything." Watkins said. "Now have a seat."

Farmer sat down.

"Tell us a little about yourself."

Instead of remaining silent, he was suddenly inclined to talk. Way too much. He spoke about how his mother wished he would die, only to later die herself. He chatted about how he believed Greg was raping kids. And then he moved onto Cagney's obsession with tattooing women's pussies. In the end, he talked so much he developed jowls.

He was preparing to tell his girlfriend's business until Watkins silenced him with the wave of a hand. "Slow down, young man."

"Wow, you certainly are a talker." Miriam laughed. "But we like that."

Farmer nodded and farted silently.

"We're glad you're in a chatty mood though." Miriam continued. "Because we have lots of questions."

"Okay…"

Miriam slid a picture across the table. "Who is this person?"

His eyes widened. When he saw the woman's face, he jumped up and vomited in the trashcan next to him. Wiping his mouth with the back of his hand he said, "Johanna." He flopped heavily back into his seat.

They looked at one another. After all, he was the first person who admitted he knew her. "How do you know her?"

Silence.

"Farmer, how do you know Johanna?" Watkins continued.

FARMER'S STORY

It was dark…

And Farmer just left his girlfriend who about an hour ago stopped him from robbing his best friend at a bar. Since he had come so close to doing what she originally said she wanted done, he grew angry when she uttered her next words.

"It's over."

"What…what do you mean?"

"I can't be bothered with you anymore, Farmer." She shrugged.

"But, you, I mean…why?"

"You're lazy. Reckless and penniless. And I'm tired of having you in my life. I could've called you on the phone, but I figured it was best to tell you to your face."

"I can't believe you are—."

"I have to go, Farmer. Bye." She walked toward her car.

He threw his arms up. "You not even gonna give me a ride home?"

"Did I bring your broke ass here? No." She unlocked her car, slid inside and drove down the street.

He was devastated.

Crushed.

Without her, he felt he had nothing.

He was a few miles up from the bar when he realized how dumb he was to think he could maintain a woman of her caliber. Although she was mean, she was also right about the state of his affairs. He needed to do better but where would he start? Outside of his job at the restaurant, he didn't have a career. He barely had a life. The only thing in his favor was that he was an extremely talented artist.

He could draw exquisitely.

But how could he market that skill?

He was so depressed that he was considering jumping in front of a moving vehicle, until he saw a pretty girl in a white car pull alongside him. She was wearing a white shirt and red tights and she was stunning.

"Where you going?" She asked.

He looked behind him and back at her. "You talking to me?"

She laughed. "Yes, silly. Where you going?"

"No...nowhere." He shrugged.

"Well do you want to come with me?"

Fifteen minutes later they were in the Marking nightclub and he felt he hit the lottery. Nothing about the moment made sense. He was waiting for Stacey to jump out and accuse him of cheating because everything felt bizarre.

Until he was reminded that she dropped him.

As the beautiful woman danced on the floor, he couldn't get over how pretty she was. Every man in the building seemed to gravitate toward her, but it was as if she only had eyes for him. As she moved her body like a snake against his frame, his dick grew rock hard. And when the last song played, she placed her lips against his ear.

"I'll be back." She whispered. "Meet me at the bar for drinks."

Considering his financial status, those words sounded like a death threat for the moment. He figured it was best to be honest. "I don't have any money."

She smiled. "Don't worry. I got you." She gave him instructions and danced away.

After ordering what she requested, the bartender wiped the bar vigorously as he eyed Farmer. "You gonna pay for these drinks or not?"

Farmer looked out into the club. "I...I mean, a girl was gonna pay for them."

He glared. "Figures."

After fifteen minutes of getting humiliated with looks from the bartender, he left the drinks where they were and went searching for the pretty stranger. After annoying several people about the girl called Johanna, he decided to walk into the woman's bathroom. Figuring that somebody that pretty, could have been taken advantage of inside. After all, she picked him up off the street and he was a total stranger.

What if she'd done the same to someone else in the club?

The moment he walked into the bathroom; he didn't see her at first. It appeared completely empty with the exception of one stall door that was open toward the back. But he had no intentions on giving up. Walking deeper inside eventually he saw her lying on the floor, with her pants down. Her purse was wide open and there was cash inside.

Since he could use the money, he grabbed it, took the bills out and dropped the bag on the floor, before running away.

BACK IN THE INTERROGATION ROOM

Watkins and Miriam looked at Farmer as he continued to tell the story. "I'm so sorry. I'm so...so sorry." Farmer cried.

"What are you sorry for?" Miriam asked. "For robbing her or killing her?"

His eyes widened. "I didn't kill her." He looked between the officers surprised. "I didn't...I didn't touch her. She was passed out. I figured she drank too much."

"That's what you say," Watkins responded. "But how do we really know that's the truth?"

Farmer felt as if he would faint. The last thing he thought he was being held for was murder. "Because she was nice. And at that moment, at that moment I really needed someone to be nice to me. So, I would never hurt someone like that."

CHAPTER 15

INTERROGATION ROOM

Greg walked into the interrogation room and flopped down in the chair. After sitting in the cell for hours he figured grabbing the little girls at the school to question them about Ocean was the reason he was there. "I need to know if my son's okay first."

"He is," Officer Miriam said. "He's in our custody right now."

"Your custody?" He frowned. "What does that mean?" His heart banged in his chest. "Because he has a mental—."

"Trust me, he's fine." Officer Watkins responded. "Which is more than I can say about you."

He felt a little better. "Okay, so, this isn't about me supposedly raping no kid is it? Because I wasn't fucking with kids. I wanted to know who did something to my son so I questioned a few students."

Watkins and Miriam looked at one another.

"Do you want to tell us something?" Officer Watkins responded sitting back.

"You know, at first, when this all happened, I realized my life was coming down around me all at once. At the same time. And it didn't make sense. But it's been this way for years which is why I moved and came back."

Watkins sighed. "Greg, let's start here." He cleared his throat. "What do you think this is about?"

He sighed. "Rasha?"

"We don't know what you're talking about."

He sighed. "Well, is it about Johanna? I think everything that has happened to me over the past couple of months has been about her. Am I right?"

"Tell us more." Miriam responded.

"About ten years ago I ran into her. I remember thinking she was the most beautiful woman I'd ever seen. I had to be around her. I had to be next to her and there was nothing anybody could tell me to convince me to change my mind."

Watkins shrugged. "Sounds like a classic young love story to me."

"I thought so too, but this was different."

"Meaning?" Miriam asked.

"One minute she was feeling me. And I could really, really tell that she wanted to be with me. And the next, the next day she would spaz out. Try to get me to fight her and when I wouldn't she would windmill me to the point where I would have to block her blows just to protect myself."

"That's what you call domestic violence these days?" Miriam asked.

He glared. "I never beat a woman straight up in my life." He pointed at them. "Ever."

"Man, do yourself a favor and put your finger down."

He did. "Like I said, I never hit a woman and I wouldn't start with Johanna. Or anybody else for that matter."

"Finish the story," Watkins said.

Greg took a deep breath. "After some time, I left her alone. I couldn't deal with her anymore. Later she came back and tells me she was pregnant. With my son Ocean. Who was three years old. But the kid was real fucked up. More messed up then he is now. And I loved that boy back to life."

"What about her?" Watkins said.

"At first she thought I would take them both back. I think she was running from somebody. And she wanted to escape through me. But after she realized I was done with her, she grew evil."

"Are you sure it's not because you were trying to keep her from her child?" Miriam asked.

"I would never keep a boy from his mother. Having a loving relationship with his mother was the only way to keep a man from being a monster."

"Was she in the boy's life or not?" Watkins asked.

He looked down. "She would say she was coming, and not show up. She would, she would say she wanted to be with him, and leave him stranded. I didn't stop her from seeing him, but I made clear that if she ever broke his heart, she would have trouble from me."

"So, you did kill her?"

"Kill her?" He looked between the both of them. "Wait, she was murdered?"

"Yes."

His eyes stretched across his face. "Now, hold up, I may have cut her off, and I may have known about her psychotic behavior, but I never would hurt the mother of my child."

"That's not what the evidence says."

CHAPTER 16
INTERROGATION ROOM

Zeno stood in the room as the detectives remained seated across from him. They demanded that he get comfortable, but the smallness of the chair made him feel crammed, and so he remained standing.

"On the way over here, I thought I knew what this was about." Zeno said. "And I didn't want to believe that someone that I deemed a son, would turn his back on me. I guess I could've handled things a bit differently. But the idea of him touching my daughter, of violating her fucks me up."

"Who are you talking about?" Watkins frowned.

"This is about Davon, right?"

They looked at one another and back at him. "No." Miriam said. "This isn't about anyone named Davon."

He frowned. "Then what is this about?"

"Johanna Howard."

"Who is that?"

"Don't play stupid, Bezeno." Watkins said with an attitude. "You and I both know you know who she is."

"I have no idea who you're talking about."

He moved closer to the table and they directed him to have a seat again, despite his earlier discomfort. This time he obliged. "If I knew who you were talking about, I would say it. Now stop the fucking games and get to the point."

Watkins slid the picture over to him. Slowly Zeno picked it up and looked at the photo. "I know this girl."

"We know you do."

"You don't understand. I know this girl from back in the day. But her name wasn't Johanna."

"We don't care when you met her. All we know is that a dead girl had your name clutched in her hand when she was murdered, along with some others. Can you explain that?"

"Nah, but if this girl is dead and my name is in the mix it means I'm being set up. And I intend on finding out who's behind this shit."

BALTIMORE COUNTY - MALE HOLDING CELL

While Zeno was being escorted back into his cell, his mind was reeling. Why was a blast from his past

240   *BY T. STYLES*

popping up now? And more importantly why was she holding his name in her palm?

As he flopped in the seat within the cell, he noticed Greg and Cagney had returned and they were all silent. Each man held the same expression, that of deep confusion. Farmer was the only person who was standing and carving on the wall, which he hadn't stopped doing since he had gotten there.

Suddenly something clicked in Zeno's mind.

"They put us in here together." Zeno said. "To fuck with us. And I'm sure we're being recorded." He looked around from where he was and couldn't find a device besides the clunky one outside the cell.

Was it strong enough to collect evidence?

"What you mean?" Greg asked. "You and I haven't seen each other in over fifteen years. Since that party."

"And still I think we are all involved." Zeno responded. "I mean, you and I both know each other from the past. It's true. But these two are probably connected somehow." Zeno rose. "Where you from?"

"East Baltimore." Greg shrugged. "You know that. But I live out the county now."

"And you?"

"Out west." Cagney responded.

"And you?"

Farmer continued to draw. "I prefer that my business stays my own."

"Nigga, answer the fucking question!" Zeno roared.

The boom in his voice caused Farmer to tremble. "From Pikesville."

Zeno examined both of them. They were younger than anybody he would've roamed with. Maybe he stomped with their fathers even though it wouldn't make sense.

"Who is your father?"

"I don't see how this matters." Cagney said scratching his belly.

"Are you being framed for murder or not?" Zeno yelled.

Maybe they were connected after all. "My pop's name is Avante."

Zeno stumbled back. And Greg's jaw dropped. They both knew him very well. Back in the day they were friends, until the night of the party when things changed. He knew the boy's face was familiar.

"And you?" He asked Farmer.

He stopped drawing and turned around. "Baines."

Greg and Zeno looked at one another. Everything clicked together like the final sections of a 1000-piece puzzle, although the picture wasn't in full view.

BY T. STYLES

But it was the drawing on the wall, that Farmer was doing, that had him shook. Slowly Zeno walked toward it and pushed Farmer to the side. "Who is this?" He pointed at it with a stiff long finger.

"Why?" Farmer frowned.

Zeno's nostrils flared. "Answer the fucking question."

To be honest he was tired of having to explain himself to the young fool. Every minute counted and they had better come together or else they could be going down together.

Possibly for life.

He swallowed. "It's my girlfriend."

Greg frowned, having finally looked at the drawing. Now he recognized the person he was bringing to life also. Although Farmer had been at it for hours, no one bothered to pay the drawing or him any mind. At the end of the day, no one cared. We see what we want to see, even when its staring us in the face.

"But I thought you said she was Asian," Greg said. "She is!"

"My nigga, this bitch ain't Asian!" Greg yelled.

"I'm sorry, is she my girlfriend or yours?"

"What the bitch is, is psycho." Greg continued. "I knew seeing that message in my son's bag meant something." He looked at Zeno.

"Now I'm confused." Cagney admitted. "Can somebody tell me what's going on?"

"Her name is Rasha." Zeno sighed.

Suddenly a guard opened the door with Watkins standing right next to him. "Let's go."

"Who?" Zeno asked.

"All of you." His jaw twitched. "Unless you want to stay here."

"But I thought I was being charged for murder." Cagney said.

"Nobody's been charged, yet. We're putting things together, so don't leave town." He pointed at them. "None of you." He sighed. "But for now, you're free to leave. I guess you have friends in high places."

Mercy walked into Sybil's room and sat on the recliner across from her bed in a quiet rage. Sybil, who had been expecting her was wide awake. The smell of

BY T. STYLES

menthol was prevalent in the air, as it made her relax. It was obvious that the old lady was very ill.

"You betrayed me, didn't you?" Mercy asked using her own voice. "You told my sister about the cops and now they've all been released."

Sybil smiled. Hearing Mercy's voice directly meant that she would soon be free to die, and she wanted this life over with. "Your sister reached out to me. And I want this all to end. You don't even know why you're doing this anymore. Is it revenge? Is it a...a game? You're no different than the boys who took advantage of you as a kid."

"Don't say that!?"

"What happened to Helena?"

"You really want to know?"

"Yes, I do."

"She got over here by a Coyote which meant she owed a debt, and I paid it off and..."

"And what else?" Sybil coughed.

"I also paid to have Laurie, her mother, sent back from Mexico."

"So, when she arrives, she'll learn her daughter is dead."

"At one time I was her only daughter. Maybe things are going back to the way they used to be."

Sybil sighed. "What was the price for you bringing her mother back, Mercy?"

"Helena's life. Nothing is free in this world."

"But Helena loved you. She loved you and you used her. Don't you realize what will happen to you now?"

"She was a snake. From the beginning. And I had a goal, and I needed her for that goal. Now she's gone."

"You have gone deeper than you can even imagine. I feel sorry for you."

She jumped up and stood over her body. "Don't feel pity for me, old woman. Feel sorry for your fucking self." She walked toward the door and came back. "And you better not die on me either."

CHAPTER 17

When Zeno, Greg, Farmer and Cagney walked out the precinct, Zeno was shocked to see Darcy standing before them. She was in her late forties, but everything was stacked together preventing those who didn't know her from guessing her real age. At the same time, she looked tired. As if life had gotten the best of her.

She and Zeno definitely had history, although based on how Zeno looked at her, none of it was good.

"Darcy, what you doing here?" Zeno asked stepping up to her, his large frame hanging over her head like a cloud.

"I got you out." She looked up at him and then the others. "I got you all out after I found out what was happening."

The men looked at one another and frowned. "I don't understand." Greg said scratching his head. "I thought you blamed us for Rasha going missing back in the day. I thought—."

"I was wrong." She took a deep breath and looked behind her. It was obvious that she felt uncomfortable. "But can we go someplace and talk? I don't like being out here in the open." She looked behind her and back at them. "It's not safe. For any of us."

An hour later they were sitting in a diner at a booth in Baltimore County. Since Zeno's body was so large, the waitress allowed them to add a chair on the side of the booth so that they all could sit together. No one was hungry so coffee cups dressed the table as they waited for what Darcy wanted to say. Before talking, she made a few texts and looked at the door, before focusing back on them.

"Darcy, what's going on?" Greg asked, looking dead into her eyes. "You gotta tell us something."

"I always thought monsters were fake. I saw movies and figured, a monster looks like this, and a monster looks like that. But never, ever, did I think a monster could look like my sister."

Zeno sat back in his seat. "We're listening."

"To put this easy, my sister wants to ruin all of your lives. In the beginning, it started as revenge against your fathers." She looked at Cagney and Farmer. "After a while, I really believe she started to enjoy being other people because she never really liked herself. And when you didn't live up to what she wanted, she tried to set you up for murder."

"I'm confused." Cagney said.

"Me too."

"Okay, to explain why my sister has lost touch with reality, let me start at the beginning."

WHAT REALLY HAPPENED AT THE HERN'S HOME
AUGUST 1988

After running from her father, Lester, Darcy was in bed with her baby sister Rasha and her brother Levyne. The lights were out, but the room still glowed, due to the streetlight in front of their home. She almost dosed off when suddenly the door opened, and Nancy hung in the doorway. Arms crossed tightly over her body as if she were enraged.

"Is everything okay?" Darcy asked. She was ready to fight the woman if she had any intentions on hurting her siblings.

Nancy shrugged. "It depends." She paused. "Who were you running from before you came here tonight? And why?"

She looked down at her soiled fingertips because she thought she made herself clear earlier.

"It was my father. Tonight, I walked in on him hanging over my baby sister's crib. Her pamper was off. And when he went to sleep, I snatched her and my brother and left." She shook her head. "But he saw me and drove after me with his car, before he got out on foot. I was able to lose him but, but I'm afraid. Afraid he will do the things he did to me to her."

"And he will. If you stay."

She nodded. "I know. Because I'm not strong enough to protect her. Not now anyway."

"You never will be."

Darcy felt dizzy, because the woman's energy didn't sit well with her from the moment she met her. "Listen, I don't wanna cause any trouble. I just wanna take care of my sister and brother for the night, until I figure out how to keep them safe."

"You think you're smart, don't you? You think you have it all together." She laughed. "You are so fucking foolish."

"I don't...I don't understand."

"You don't know what it's like to live a life on the streets. Of having to run from home to home. And you don't know the damage you can do on her young mind if you pull her into that lifestyle."

Darcy looked back at her baby sister and then the woman. "I...I..."

"I'll tell you what'll happen." She stepped closer. "You will fail. And when that happens, she will fall to the streets and it will be all your fault. Don't get me wrong." She shrugged. "It's possible that she will ease into that one percent and will make it out okay. And meet a man like Joe." She nodded toward the door. "Like I did when my sister abandoned me. But the road to a man like that will be long and hard. And you will ruin her life."

Darcy was horrified. Her young mind wasn't built to deal with a conniving woman like Nancy. And as a result, she started doubting everything she was doing. "So, what can I do?"

"Leave. Let me take care of her."

Her eyes widened. "But I can't...I..."

ASK THE STREETS FOR MERCY   251

"Or maybe I'll call the police instead." She lowered her brow. "And tell them that you ran away from home. Maybe they'll put you all in a foster home together. Or maybe they will separate you, like they did with me and my sister."

"Please don't call the police."

"So, go. Take your brother. And let me raise her in a good home."

Darcy cried softly. "But I don't want to leave my —."

"I will provide her with the life you can't. Trust me. It's better this way."

Her head shook slowly from left to right. Slowly she turned around and looked at her sister. Suddenly her eyes widened, and a smile dressed her face. "Can I come see her? That way, that way she will know me?"

"No. She has to rely on me to take care of her. And with you around, she won't be able to do that."

"But if I leave, she will, she'll hate me."

"I will make sure that she knows you did this for love." She lied. "I will make sure she knows how much you care about her. Leave her a note. And I'll take care of the rest."

"What do I write?"

"Write what you feel."

Later on that night, heartbroken and viscerally ill, Darcy penned a note to Rasha's shirt, took her little brother and left the Hern home. But her plan was never to leave her forever.

And at the same time what Nancy said resonated with her spirit.

If she was going to save her sister, I mean truly save her, she had to make sure she could prepare a way. First, she went back to her father's apartment with her little brother. However, she threatened him in a major way.

"If you ever touch me again, or my brother, I will tell them everything you did to me."

"Where is my daughter?"

"Don't worry about that. She's safe. But did you hear what I said?" She trembled. It was the first time she stood up to him.

Lester glared down at her. "You little bitch. You can stay here because you're underage and I don't want to pay child support, but I will never love you. And I will only do the basics. In other words, you're on your own."

Darcy didn't care. She braided hair on the side to provide food for herself and her brother. Ironically enough, Lester helped himself to their food because the bounty was so plentiful.

Darcy was a good caregiver and she didn't mind. Just as long as he left her and her brother alone.

Instead, she did well in school, worked hard. But she never got over Rasha being with a family she didn't know. And every day she missed her and cried herself to sleep, hoping that Rasha was okay. Over time she befriended a teacher at school. The woman was so impressed with how hard Darcy worked, that when she told her about Rasha living with the Hern family, who up until that point was caring for her illegally, along with the tales of her father's sexual abuse, the teacher vowed to help by bringing the siblings into her home. Darcy, excited, boasted to Lester that she would be leaving him soon.

The next day the teacher died in a car accident.

And Darcy always felt like he was responsible.

With her death, before she could be reunited with her sister, Darcy would have to wait until she was of age. She had no idea that the Hern's had fallen for the little girl hard and did all they could to keep her in their lives. Including going to CPS, claiming that the child was abandoned. After a few months, when no one claimed Rasha, they were granted full custody.

The rest was history.

In the beginning both Nancy and Joe did all they could do to care for Rasha, but it was Joe who Rasha gave her whole heart too, which caused Nancy to feel extreme isolation and abandonment. To some her pain was justified. Besides, Joe was barely home during the earlier years. It was Nancy who nursed Rasha when she was sick, dressed her in the prettiest outfits and hugged her when she was sad.

So, when Nancy overheard Rasha telling Joe that she didn't like her, she saw black. And before long, Nancy accepted her rejection and delivered it back as hate.

No matter what was going on in the Hern home, Darcy would not be content until she could be reunited with her sister. And so, six years later, when she became an adult, she decided to get full custody. It was only during that time, after going to CPS, that Darcy learned that the Hern's claimed they didn't know Rasha had family.

It didn't matter. She was her flesh and blood. And so, she went to the Hern's home vowing to be reunited with Rasha. "I came for my sister."

Joe, who had fallen for the child would never give her up. "I don't know who you are, but my daughter isn't going anywhere."

She frowned. What was he saying? She had sat on his sofa. In the exact same house. "What do you mean you don't know who I am?"

"Like I said, I don't know who you are." He stared her in the eyes. "And never come to my home again." He slammed the door in her face.

But that wouldn't be the end for Darcy. She kept on the police until they decided to go to the Hern's home about Rasha.

But the Hern's were ready for her the next time.

"Rasha is my sister and I want to take her with me!" Darcy yelled, crying at the doorway with the authorities and a social worker at her side.

Again, he opened the door. "Like I told the CPS, we found Rasha on the side of the road." Joe responded. "And we took care of her, when no one wanted her. But we did do a background check on you."

Darcy's eyes widened.

"You have a prescription drug habit." Joe said. "You had it honestly, since your mother also abused pain pills. I heard your brother went away to military school, but when he was younger, you gave drugs to him too. Didn't you?"

There was the dark part of Joe Hern's that Darcy also saw when she first met him.

Still, he was right.

Darcy recalled the moment she first met them, when she popped a pill in Levyne's mouth to calm his nerves. She wasn't trying to be malicious. She loved her little brother. But she was doing what she learned from her mother. And now it could be the reason she was kept apart from Rasha.

After hearing about the drug abuse, the social worker looked at Darcy. "Is that true?"

Silence.

"Is it true, young lady?" One of the officers asked.

Darcy looked down. "Yes, but I'm getting better and—."

"I don't know what's going on here," the caseworker said. "But if we find out drugs are in your system; we won't allow you to get custody. And that information will remain on Rasha's file. And it will ruin any chance of you ever being able to take care of Rasha in the future. Is that what you want?"

"No." She shook her head slowly.

There were probably drugs in her system. After all, she led a dark life leading up to that moment. She had done many things to keep her brother safe and food on the table. Some of the things Nancy warned her would happen to Rasha, happened to her instead, but the other things she discovered along the way.

So, for now she would have to wait.

A few months later, she returned to the caseworker's office and made a simple plea. "If my father agrees to take my sister back, would you let her stay with him?"

Mrs. Sharpley sat back in her leather seat and rocked a little. "Why won't you let this go?"

"Because at first I thought the Hern's were nice people. But why would nice people keep me away from my sister? I mean, he is her biological parent. Don't you have an obligation to reunite them?"

She sighed. "But I thought you didn't trust your father."

Silence.

"Darcy, I thought you said you didn't trust him."

"I was young. And maybe I remember things incorrectly."

She stopped rocking and placed her forearms on the desk. "So, you lied on him? Is that what you're telling me?"

She nodded yes.

"How do you know he will want to take care of her. Maybe he has a new family now and—."

"Because I'll be there. So, he'll have help."

She frowned. "But you just moved into your own place." She scanned through the file on her desk. "Or am I crazy? You were even going to bring Rasha to your apartment if we gave you custody. So—."

"I did move to my own apartment. But…but if you let him have her, I'll be there for her. I promise."

The following day she went to visit her father. It was one of the hardest things she'd ever had to do, especially since she knew he was a monster.

When she went to his house, he was having drinks with a man who smelled of trash, and she wondered if this was her worst idea yet. "What do you want, Darcy? You got five minutes."

Looking down she said, "CPS won't let me have Rasha."

He shrugged. "Why not? You're grown. Even got your own place." He chuckled once. "At least that's what you kept throwing up in my face."

"I, I mean…"

Suddenly things made sense. Putting his drink on the table he pointed her way. "They know about the drugs, don't they?"

She nodded yes.

He laughed heavily. "And you talk about me."

"Please."

"Welp, I have a life now. Don't much have space for a teenager." He grabbed his drink and guzzled most of it down. "Got a girl too. Maybe we'll move out of here and get a place of our own."

She stepped closer. "Daddy, I'll take care of her. I'll, I'll take care of you too."

He laughed. "What makes you think I want you anywhere near me?" He frowned. "I mean look at you. You hardly pretty anymore. Your body's already falling apart, and you look like, life has gotten a hold of you."

"Daddy, I'll do everything in the bedroom I didn't do before."

Upon her saying those words, he looked at his friend and back at her. He started to deny everything. But there was no use in him trying to fake it. Everybody knew about Nasty Lester. "Still don't mean I'd want to be bothered with you or that stank pussy of yours."

"I'll make it worth your while. As long as you leave my sister alone." Darcy was smarter than she let on. The plan was to take Rasha out of the home the moment she crossed the threshold. But she didn't want him to know that. "Please."

Despite Lester's attitude, for some reason he agreed to let Rasha stay in his home. But things didn't go as smoothly as she hoped, because once returning to the

Hern's home with the caseworker and police, she learned that Rasha had been taken away. It took some work, but after some time, Darcy located Laurie while she was at the grocery store alone.

"I know you have my sister." She said as they stood in the meat aisle. "If you don't give her to me, I will ruin your life."

"I don't know what you're —."

"I know where you live too, Laurie. And if you were trying to help my sister, I'm grateful. But I'm older now. And I want to bring her home. You have two days."

After that conversation, Laurie made plans to leave Rasha where Darcy could get her at the grocery store. Besides, Helena was back, and she wanted to focus all of her attention on her own child.

Little did she know her daughter would let Rasha know, which resulted in Rasha calling the police instead. Causing Laurie to be taken back to Mexico due to an expired Visa.

It didn't matter though. Because in the end, Rasha would finally be brought to Darcy, except she didn't get the warm reception she thought she would receive. As a matter of fact, she didn't get a reception at all.

As Rasha stood in the hallway with her social worker, Darcy was inside waiting. Finally, she would be reunited after locating her at the maid's house a little while back. After all, she had been fighting for this moment all her life.

The social worker looked down at Rasha when they approached number 34B. "You'll be fine. I know he wants to meet you."

Rasha clutched her suitcase which had the doll's head sticking from the zipper in one hand, and her chalkboard in the other.

When the door opened Lester was on the other side. But someone else was inside too. It was Darcy, standing in the kitchen with a smile on her face.

She waited a lifetime for this moment.

"Mr. Dupree," Mrs. Sharpley started. "How are you?"

He nodded. "Is this her?"

"Yes, sir, this is your child."

He nodded. "Ugly. Unlike her mama." He looked at her legs. "Built strong though." He licked his lips.

Mrs. Sharpley cleared her throat. "May we come in. I have some things to go over with you before I leave."

Once the duo was inside, Darcy waved at Mrs. Sharpley and she waved back, although it was with annoyance. She didn't care for Darcy after she bugged the woman for so long to be reunited with her sister. But it wasn't about her. It was about the sisters.

However, when Darcy waved at Rasha, she looked away.

After a few more words, the social worker said, "Can I see where she'll be staying?"

He scratched his beard and it crackled like popcorn. "Come with me."

When they disappeared into the back of the apartment Darcy sat next to Rasha. "How are you?"

Rasha remained silent as her eyes rested on some things longer than others because she had selective memory and selective focus, choosing only to recognize those things that created the picture she desired.

"Rasha, I know you're mad at me. But I never gave up trying to find you. I never gave up fighting for you. And I know you hate me, but—."

Rasha looked at her.

It was a look so cold, she wished she'd never looked at her again. Afraid of her flesh and blood, Darcy stood up and backed against the wall. Nothing about her felt innocent or pure.

When Mrs. Sharpley and Lester returned to the living room the social worker smiled at Rasha. "Well, everything looks good. I think you'll like it here. You'll have plenty of company." She looked at Darcy who was still staring at her sister as if she'd seen the devil himself. "Well, I'll have to go." She shook Lester's hand. "Call if you need anything."

Days later, after getting over the initial shock, every day for the time they spent in the apartment together, Darcy tried her best to connect emotionally with her sister. But nothing worked. She wouldn't speak to her. She wouldn't look at her. It had become clear that maybe Rasha had convinced herself that Darcy wasn't there.

That Darcy was dead.

More like a ghost.

But still Darcy was resilient. Even taking to warning her about the sexual appetite of their father even while she treated her as if she were not listening.

One day while they were in the bedroom they shared, Darcy walked over to her and sat next to her on the bed.

"Listen, you don't have to speak to me, but you can't be alone with daddy. He's not a nice man. He'll take advantage of you. And maybe even hurt you if you let him. You must be careful."

Unlike the first time they were reunited, this time Rasha didn't look at her. Her ability to do this was so strong, she wondered if she were hypnotized out of her life.

Despite being ignored, Darcy continued to provide blockage between her sister and her father. When he was horny Darcy would have sex with him. When he was drunk, she would lay in the doorway, and go to his bed before he reached her sister's bed.

But that wasn't enough.

He wanted Rasha and he was growing weary of not having her.

One Night Rasha had prepared hot dogs for Lester. Darcy offered to cook instead after realizing he was drunk, but Lester had taken to ignoring her when Rasha was around, almost as if he were trying to appease her and hurt Darcy's feelings.

It worked.

Darcy watched her sister write on her chalkboard: I GRILLED THE BUNS.

He opened one of the hot dogs and grinned. "Yep, you sure did, my special girl."

A chair moved. Because Darcy slammed down in her seat.

And still they ignored her.

Instead, Rasha and Lester communicated with each other while Darcy remained in the room. As if she weren't there. Still, she saw the lustful look in Lester's eyes. She knew her efforts to protect her sister using her own body was weakening.

So, she had to act.

Later that night, while standing up, swaying and drunk, Lester said to Rasha, "Come over here. Dance with me."

A plate fell off the table. Because Darcy knocked it off the table.

Still they ignored her.

Eager to please, Rasha jumped up and wrapped her arms around her father. And Darcy lost her mind upon seeing the embrace. There was no way she would allow him to rape her sister. She'd kill him first.

"I know what you're doing! And I'm going to call the police! Do you hear me? I'm going to call the police!"

"Shut up!" He yelled at Darcy. "Just, just shut up!" He looked down at Rasha as she ran into his arms. And then when the music slowed, he pulled her closer.

Closer than a father should be holding his daughter.

From where Darcy stood, she could see his penis growing and knew she had to do something. So, thinking quickly on her feet, Darcy called his girlfriend in the bedroom on the phone.

Sitting on the edge of the bed with the handset glued to her ear she said, "Tiffany, I know we don't have much of a relationship."

"That's your fault not mine. You haven't liked me since the day you moved back in."

It was true.

"I know. It's just that, I guess, anybody dealing with my father I don't have much respect for."

"At least you speaking the truth. Now what do you want?"

"As you know I care about my sister a lot."

"It's the only thing you care about. Following her around like some kind of shadow. Do you even have a life?"

"She is my life. And I'm concerned about her right now."

"What you saying?"

Silence.

"Darcy, if you want me to help, you have to tell me what you're saying."

"I think he may be about to rape her." She looked down. "Can you come over? Please?"

"He wouldn't do that. He's a good—."

"He did it to me. And I know you believe me. Please help my little sister."

She remained silent for a few moments and said, "I'm on my way."

When the fourth song came on the radio in the living room, Lester was minutes from pulling Rasha into the bedroom until there was a knock at the door.

Angry at the interruption, he walked toward it and opened it wide. It was Tiffany, his girlfriend. Without wasting time, he pulled her inside and kissed her sloppily, essentially forgetting all about Rasha instantly.

Coming up for breath he asked, "What you doing here, Tiffany? Thought you couldn't hang out because you had to get up early for work in the morning."

She looked toward the table, where Darcy sat, and then back at her boyfriend. "True. But I still wanted to stop by. I guess I missed you."

Later on, that night, Lester told Rasha she received a letter and went to the bedroom with his girl. Taking the letter off the counter, Rasha walked outside and flopped on the steps. After reading its contents, the letter floated out of her hand and fell to her feet. Suddenly there was a cool breeze on her back. Because Darcy had come outside.

Irritated with her presence, Rasha glared.

And there was a breeze at her back again. Because Darcy had walked back inside.

Darcy knew then that Rasha would hate her forever, and that trying to save her life would take more work than she imagined. But it didn't mean she would stop trying.

Even if it meant her life.

PRESENT DAY
THE DINER

Darcy took a break from telling the story to take a deep breath. Looking over at Zeno, Cagney, Greg and Farmer she said, "I'm sorry I'm stopping right here. But this is, this is hard."

"Based on what you said, what does any of this gotta do with us?" Cagney asked.

Just at that moment Sable walked inside. Seeing her from afar, Darcy stood up and waved her over to the table, while the fellas wondered who the dominate girl was. She was also wearing fresh pants.

"Please don't tell me that's Rasha," Farmer said.

"It's not," Darcy took her seat. "And Rasha goes by Mercy now."

Sable shook her hand and the waitress brought over another chair. "Sorry it took me so long. Had to change clothes. You must be Darcy?"

"I am." She sighed.

"Thank you for getting me out." She looked around the table. "But can you explain what's happening?"

Darcy looked at Zeno and Greg. "This is Kadir's daughter, her name is Sable." She paused. "And you've already met Baines' son Farmer. And Avante's son Cagney."

Zeno and Greg glanced at one another again. They knew Sable looked familiar. She literally had his whole face.

"Me and Greg used to run with all of your fathers back in the day." Zeno responded. "This is, this is crazy."

Sable looked down and looked back at Darcy. "And how did you know my father, Darcy?"

"My connection is all about the party and my sister." Darcy looked at Zeno. "Do you want to tell them about that night, or should I?"

He dragged a heavy hand down his face. "Naw, I'll do it."

THE NIGHT OF THE PARTY

Tired of staying at Zeno's apartment without him or his mother, Rasha slipped through the door of the party at her cousin's house. She realized that although the music was loud, the lights were dim, but no one was dancing.

Instead, the couch was propped in the center of the living room. And everyone sat in different places on the floor, with their wide eyes glued onto the television. There wasn't an empty spot available.

Easing behind the crowd, as she focused on the glow from the television on their faces, she followed their stares. Her heart dropped when she saw what appeared to be an amateur movie, starring herself.

With her heart beating like thunder, first she saw long shots of her sitting alone across the street on the step. While Kadir and Nalo spoke about how she would be their next victim.

The film continued with her being forced under the water at the pool by Kadir while Nalo laughed while holding the camera. Prior to that moment, she didn't even realize he was present.

Next using night vision, the movie followed her into the haunted house, only to be terrorize by Nalo. While tears streamed down her face, she heard the roar of laughter from everyone present.

If that wasn't enough, they even had video of her being arrested for shoplifting, along with the video of Greg stealing her father's car, only for her to run toward the vehicle in an attempt to take back the keys.

Oh, how they all laughed.

Loudly.

And at her expense.

But the animals had yet to truly showcase their depravity.

"Shhhhh," Kadir announced to all the movie watchers. "This is the good part."

Because in came the video of her being raped in the backseat of the car. Since her juice had been spiked, she didn't know who was there when she blacked out.

But now she did.

Each one of them took turns holding the camera while they videotaped the act and she found herself feeling queasy looking at the footage. Uncaring and cold, each of them took the time to point the camera to their own faces. It was Kadir, Nalo, Baines and Avante, and they took turns violating her body.

At the end of the day she was the butt of the joke and as she looked around and saw everyone laughing at her pain, and calling her whores, she became filled with rage.

It was obvious.

They wanted to ruin her life.

And something happened in that moment. As she saw her own face riddled with pain, she could honestly see that she was just a child. And she wondered what would have happened if someone put their children under the same mental stress.

Would they be able to survive?

"What are you doing here?" Greg asked walking up behind her, so that only she could hear him. He smelled of alcohol and although it was late, she could see that his eyes were bloodshot red.

She pointed at the TV. It was at that time that she realized he was the only one who wasn't on the tape during the rape.

"Oh, uh, come with me." He giggled.

What was funny?

She pointed at the TV again, with her trembling hand but stiff finger.

"Come with me and I'll tell you everything you want to know."

When he led her toward the back of the apartment, she was irritated that his laughter grew louder. It was obvious he knew something she didn't and once again it was plain to see that they didn't care about her emotions.

After all, what was funny?

Her world was crashing down around her and it was on full display. She felt like she was in a nightmare and didn't even know where he was taking her. But when the door opened, she saw where the joke lied. Because Zeno was on top of Helena, on the bed, kissing her passionately.

Devastated once again, Rasha stumbled backward and slammed against the dresser, as Greg balled over laughing at hemming Zeno up. Although he didn't realize Rasha knew Helena, he did know that Zeno was Rasha's boyfriend.

"Why you bring her in here, man?" Zeno yelled getting out of bed and sliding into his sweatpants.

Greg couldn't respond because he was laughing so hard. Being mean was a way of life for him and his friends. And so was being drunk, which he was at the moment. Greg's reason for bringing Rasha in the room was simple. He and his friends were sick of him butting into the business, when it came to Rasha. And so, he wanted their bond destroyed.

"Rasha, I'm so sorry!" Helena said grabbing a sheet to cover her body. "Please forgive me! I was bored at Sybil's and—"

"Wait, you know her?" Zeno asked glaring down at her. "I, I didn't know."

Rasha's mind was reeling as she tried to understand what was happening. All she could do was run out crying.

PRESENT DAY
BACK AT THE DINER

Everyone sat back in their chairs and looked at Zeno. "I was young, but I loved Rasha. And I didn't find out until later that she knew Helena."

Cagney, Sable and Farmer all looked at one another.

"After the party she went missing, and they assumed I did something to her." Zeno looked across the table. "Especially Darcy."

"I'm so sorry," she said. "I didn't know the details until I researched what happened later. But why didn't you tell me about the movie until now?"

"Listen, I didn't even know they were taping that shit." Zeno shrugged. "Or that they were showing it to the world. I was there for a party, met Helena who used to walk around the neighborhood at night, and one thing led to another. My only crime was taking her to the room. That's it." He looked at Greg. "You should never had brought her in there when you knew I had a chick in there with me."

"I know, man. I was young and drunk. Plus, whenever we tried to talk to her, you got in the way so..." It all sounded so dumb now and as a result, he couldn't even finish his sentence.

"I get it, but what you and them niggas did started all of this shit." Zeno continued.

"Whatever happened at that party is just the tip of what's going on at this point." Darcy said. "I knew my sister was dark, but I didn't realize the depravity she would reach later in life until I had her followed." She looked at Sable. "I'm pretty sure she had everything to do with killing your father."

Her eyebrows rose. "He committed suicide. Jumped off the top of his apartment building."

"Don't believe that, Sable. I mean, I don't have proof, but I'm sure she was responsible." Darcy sighed deeply.

She felt like she was betraying her sister, but she was concerned for them all. She was concerned for the world. And with her sister roaming around, she was concerned for herself too.

"Rasha went through a lot. It's true. Had a lot of bad things happen to her. But she had a lot of good things happen too. There were many people who helped her in life, but she only focuses on the things that didn't go her way. And she never forgives. Even though she wears that cross around her neck."

"So, what does that mean for us?" Sable said. "We wasn't involved in that party shit."

"I know. But she doesn't care." She reached into her pocket and pulled out a picture of Helena and showed them all.

"That's Johanna," each of them said. After all, they all had interactions with the same woman and was being looked at for her murder.

Greg, who only laid eyes on Helena briefly the night of the party when he was a child, didn't realize until that moment that the mother of his child was the same person. Instead of angering Zeno even more, he decided that for now, he'd keep that piece of information to himself.

"Her name is Helena." Darcy said. "And my sister used this girl because she knew she wanted her mother back in the country."

"So, this girl would kill herself just to bring her mother back?" Farmer asked.

"Yes. She slit her own throat at the club. But before she did, she made sure that each of your names were on a piece of paper clutched in her palm."

"Can I see a picture of your sister?" Farmer asked. "Because when I drew my girl on the wall, Greg and Zeno seemed to believe that she's the same person."

She looked down. "She was standing across the street when you all came out of the precinct. At least I think that was her. It's amazing because she's both ugly and beautiful at the same time. With the ability to become a chameleon." She scrolled through her phone. "But this is the only photo I have of her, from two years back." She placed it on the table. "I took it when she was at a diner when she didn't know I was there. Could've cost me my life."

Farmer stared at it the longest. "That's her. That's my girlfriend."

Sable looked at it and her jaw dropped. "That's, that's my girlfriend too."

Everybody began to talk at the same time, and it was clear that Mercy worked long and hard to ruin lives.

It was Cagney's time to look at the picture. When he saw her face, his jaw dropped. "This is, this is my boss. From the tattoo shop. And at one time I dated her, but she drove me crazy."

For a moment they all took the time to look at one another.

Darcy sighed again. "By now you know how serious this is. Up until this point, she's been playing games. Now things are serious. And there is no use in trying to find her after tonight. She will abandon the fake identities and try something more dangerous. I suggest you leave town if you can but don't go back to your old places."

"But we live together." Sable said mainly to herself. "You want me to believe that she will just walk away?"

"Yes! She was playing the long con. Fucking with you was her way of gaining some of the power back she believes your fathers took away from her when she was younger."

"Well why not mess with them?" Farmer said. "Why bother us?"

"She did." She paused. "Like I said, I believe she killed Kadir, Nalo is locked up and I hear she has him tortured on the regular."

"And my father is out here on drugs," Cagney said looking down.

"Exactly, which I know for a fact she got him on. And Baines is in hiding." Darcy sighed. "Which is even more reason why she turned her attention to their sons. And Zeno..." She looked at him closer. "You need to pay close attention to your baby mother Juno."

He moved uneasily since his mother already told him to beware earlier. But more than anything she knew her name. "So, what happens now?" Zeno asked.

"Pay attention to everything and everybody. And when she finds you, and she will, contact me. I will know what to do."

"How did you stop them from charging us?" Farmer asked.

"Joe left me some money too after he died." She sighed. "From guilt I'm sure. Anyway, I made a few moves in real estate and hired good detectives.

280   *BY T. STYLES*

Eventually I located a good friend of my sister. And the rest became clear." She sighed. "So, like I said, we need to stick together and —."

Zeno stood up. "Naw."

She looked up at him. "Naw what?"

"I'm going to find her on my own." He paused. "Now since all of this has come to light, I'm sure she ruined my life in other ways, and I won't play games with her anymore."

"If you go at it alone it will be your biggest mistake." Darcy responded. "We are stronger together. Trust me."

"Why?"

"Because we are alive. She has killed others. That means she's still enjoying fucking with your minds. It's that simple."

"I'm gonna tell you what I'm going to do, I'm going to find her and kill the bitch. And when I do, I'll hit you so you can scoop the body."

"No, you won't."

"Fuck you talking about?"

"You won't be able to do any of that because you're still in love with her. Even after everything she did to you. It's all in your eyes."

"You don't know me as much as you think you do. But let's see what happens when I drop her flesh at your feet."

She grabbed his hand softly. "I understand your rage. Just, just think about calling me before you do anything. Please."

He pulled his hand back and walked away.

PRESENT DAY - MERCY'S

When Mercy walked through her bedroom with an attitude, Palmer was on her heels. Closing the door behind himself he said, "Is it true?"

She grabbed her phone and texted: **NOT NOW.**

He snatched it from her hand and flung it across the room. "Don't fucking play with me! Is it true that you've been pretending to be all these different people? When you were gone for days, telling me you were doing research. Was you leading other lives?"

She went for the phone again and he grabbed her by the wrist. "Use your voice for once! I'm sick of this other shit. I've dealt with it for years! Talk to me!"

She looked down. The thought of talking directly to him in anyway, terrorized her. She really believed that her words were evil when she spoke to a person and so she never wanted to talk directly to those she cared about.

As he looked upon her, he could see the fear of losing him in her eyes. She shook her head and he pulled her into his arms. "It'll be okay, Mercy. But I need you to talk to me. Because if you don't, I'm about to walk out on you forever."

She stepped away from him. Opening her mouth slowly she closed it once more. And then she said, "If you die, I will make sure your funeral is a closed casket for what you're making me do."

He sighed. "I'll be fine. Talk to me directly."

She looked down. "I had to do what I had to do, Palmer. I had to become those different people so I could get into their minds, and fuck things up."

"But you had Helena for that!"

Silence.

"Mercy, why get involved when you had Helena for the job?" He paused. "Tell me something."

She took a deep breath and slowly her head rose. "Maybe I liked it."

CHAPTER 18

After leaving the diner, Darcy went to pick up her five-year-old son from the sitter's. Before she walked inside, she got a text message from Greg saying he grabbed his son and he was moving back out of town. Knowing her sister well, she wished him luck, believing it was a smart move.

The moment she pulled up at the house, even though things looked okay, she felt as if something was wrong. A few minutes later she walked up the stairs and through the entrance.

The door was wide open.

Walking into the living room that was littered with toys, she saw her sister sitting on a recliner stroking her son's curly hair. Where was her babysitter? Where were all the kids?

More than anything, what stung her was the fact that Rasha was staring directly at her. And she'd followed her sister enough to know that meant one thing.

She was about to die.

"Rasha, please don't hurt my—."

Mercy squeezed her son's arm and he cried out in pain, the whole time she had a smile on her face.

BY T. STYLES

Darcy took one step closer and extended her palms. "I'm begging you." She trembled. "That is your nephew. He's your flesh and blood. Please...please don't hurt my son."

"Then don't disrespect my name. Now who am I?"

"Mercy!"

She stopped applying pressure. "You wanted to meet me. You wanted me to see you. Now I'm here." She glared. "So tell me, why are you so quiet my dear sister?"

Darcy was so afraid urine released from her body and ran down her inner thigh. "Listen, I, I know you're angry, And I understand that—."

"You don't know anything about me! You don't know anything about what I've been through. You left me! You left me to go through hell and you didn't care! And now when I seek to take back what was taken from me, you choose their sides?"

"Mercy, you're right. I did leave you, but it wasn't because I wanted to. I left you because daddy was about to rape you. So I wanted you to be some place safe, until I could come back for you." She placed a hand over her heart. "But I swear, the plan was always to come back for you."

"You should've stayed out of it." She sat back in the seat and stroke her nephew's hair again. His body remained stiff. "Because I'm no longer a victim."

"So, you like harming people who had nothing to do with what happened to you?"

Mercy smiled.

"What you're doing must stop." She put a hand over her heart. "And I know you'll have to answer to your crimes. But I will be there with you every step of the way. I'll let them all know what you've been through. I promise."

"Have you noticed you hear my voice, dear sister?"

She nodded. "Yes."

"Do you know what that means?"

She swallowed the lump in her throat. "Yes, Mercy."

Shoving the baby off of her lap, she jumped up as the child ran away. Within seconds, Darcy and Mercy clashed on the floor, as the two of them began fighting for their lives.

Mercy grabbed at Darcy's hair, while Darcy tried her best to hold her so that she wouldn't strike her. Even through it all, she didn't want to injure her baby sister, but things reached a different level when Mercy used her thumbs in an attempt to poke out her eyes.

In the end, when Darcy realized how violent she was about to become, she decided to fight back. Blow after blow they landed on each other. Darcy was getting the best of her until Rasha pulled out a box cutter in an attempt to shred her face.

The tip of the blade was inches from her face when Mercy saw flashing red and blue lights shining on the house from outside. Her eyes widened.

Standing up she said, "You...you called the police?"

"The moment I pulled up and felt something was off." She said out of breath.

"You're going to see me again." She pointed at her with the boxcutter. "That much I promise." She ran out the back door.

CHAPTER 19

Mercy was in Sybil's hospital room, as she watched her while she was asleep. Although she had known pain as a child, she never experienced pain as deep as what she was going through now. The thought of losing the old lady hit differently, and she was sure if she died, she would never come back out of this unscathed. She was unconscious but it didn't stop Mercy from brushing her hair. It was something she'd done when Sybil was awake, which she loved.

She was just about to break down when Palmer walked through the door. "How you doing, baby?"

She ran up to him and wrapped her arms around him. "They not sure how much longer she has."

He kissed her on the top of the head and held her tighter. "She'll be fine, Mercy. Trust me."

"I should never have talked to her. I should have never talked directly to her. I know my voice is poison. And now, now I talked to you too. It's—."

"Listen, stop all that nonsense." He separated from her. "You aren't a witch with death on your tongue. You will be fine. We will be fine. And Sybil is strong. She can pull through this I know she can."

She sighed and suddenly she thought about the things Sybil represented. Peace. Forgiveness and love. She had seen Mercy do a lot of evil things to a lot of people, and always held on to hope that she would change.

She started to wonder if maybe she could.

"I saw my sister the other day."

He frowned. "You talked directly to her?"

She nodded.

"How was it?"

"I don't know. It wasn't good and we fought. But it was almost like a dream because I felt like I was seeing her for the first time. It's like, I, I hate her. But I want to, I want to try to let go. But how do you let go of something you hate so much?"

Palmer gripped her in his arms. He had always seen strength in her, even when he saw her on the streets as a girl. And he knew that she was capable of change if she only tried.

"You can do it."

"But I'm afraid."

"I got you, Mercy. I got us. Just trust me."

He spent twenty more minutes in the room before standing up and kissing her on the lips. "Okay, I have to meet the fellas. I'll be back later on tonight." He walked toward the door.

"Palmer." She said.

He stopped and turned around to face her. "Yes, baby?"

"I...I..." She wanted to say I love you, but she was afraid of what the words really meant for her soul.

"I already know." He winked and walked out the door.

The moment he made a left out of the hospital and walked into the parking lot, he was grabbed from behind by three men. When he was taken to a silver van and tossed inside, he was shocked to see Zeno.

His life flashed before his eyes, as he thought about Mercy. He thought about his family. And he thought about making her speak to him.

Did forcing her to do so, really mean he sealed his fate?

"What do you want with me, nigga?" Palmer yelled out of breath. He knew exactly who he was, as he helped Mercy with her original plan to ruin his life.

"Don't worry, my nigga." He leaned closer. "You about to find out."

Mercy's nerves were bad as she texted multiple people trying to find out where Palmer was. In all of the years that they'd been together he never once not answered her call. He never once not showed up or came home at night. So she knew something immediately was off.

She felt that a move was being made on her squad, and so she had to act fast. Unwilling to sit by and let people destroy the rest of her life, she picked up her phone and texted her next man in line in The Oxford's.

IT'S TIME TO GO AWF.

Cagney heard all he needed to hear at the diner from Darcy. If the woman he came in contact with over the years was that crazy, he decided to be smart and get out of town. And so, he needed to grab his laptop from the tattoo shop, along with the little money he had stashed under the floorboard in the bathroom and leave town. The way he saw it was simple, he was not about to die for his father's evil ways.

After collecting everything he came for at the shop, he was preparing to walk out when he turned around and saw members of The Oxfords, along with Mercy standing before him. He shook his head.

Running a hand down his face he said, "Your sister told me not to come back."

She glared. The fact that her sister inserted herself into her plans, angered her even more. "So why didn't you listen?"

He looked down. "I don't know. But it looks like it will be the stupidest decision of my life." He sighed. "Can I ask you a question? Why do all of this? Why play games? And pretend to be my boss and all of this stupid shit."

"Maybe you should ask your father."

She removed her weapon. A beautiful silver .45 with a pearl handle and aimed at him. "Any last words?"

He started to say something profound. Something that would represent how he felt. And at the same time, after speaking to Darcy he knew none of that would matter. And so, holding his head high he said, "Yeah, you can suck my —."

Before he could finish his sentence, a bullet ripped through his chest as he dropped to the floor. She watched until life was drained from his eyes.

Sable was in bed with Hunter thinking about her life over the past few years. She always felt like Ebony played mental games, but she never understood why. Even after Darcy explained the gravity of her sister's sick level of revenge, she wondered if maybe Darcy was going too far.

Maybe she wasn't that bad.

"So, what do you think will happen now?" Hunter asked as she was tucked in front of her laying down.

"I don't know." She kissed the back of her shoulder. "Based on what happened to her I can understand why she would be mad at my father. But why is she bothering me?"

"Maybe that's what Darcy meant. It sounds to me that she uses revenge as an excuse to play games. Just like the people who videotaped and raped her."

"I feel like when we were together, we were really in a relationship. But I also felt like she wanted me to cheat, so that I could prove her right. Like she needed me to be bad so it could prove I was evil. But now I—."

The alarm sounded off causing them to pop up in bed. "Somebody's here." Sable whispered. "We have to—"

Before they could make an escape three men along with Mercy entered the bedroom. Sable was surprised because she had Ebony's face, but her eyes were darker. She looked as if she were someone else.

"Ebony, why—."

"By now you know that's not my name." She aimed her gun.

"Please don't hurt her," Sable begged. "She had nothing to do with—"

"You see this barrel pointing your way, and the only thing you want is to save this whore?"

Hunter wept quietly in the background.

"Why do this?" Sable asked. "Was it really revenge?"

She smiled. "I did it because I fucking wanted to."

Sable glared. "Did you kill my father?"

She laughed. "Fuck you think?" And let loose several bullets, leaving them both slumped on the bed.

When Avante approached Baines outside next to Baines' car, he seemed desperate and on edge. Baines was very irritated. After all, they agreed not to see one another unless it was an emergency. Mainly because all of their lives at one point or another they always felt like Rasha was near. After all, they'd seen what happened to their friends and now their children. So, they had to be careful.

Standing on the sidewalk Avante said, "She's back! She's fucking back and I thought we wouldn't have to deal with this anymore!"

Baines felt sick. "How do you know? It's been over fifteen years."

"Have you spoken to your son?" Avante asked.

"No, it's been years." He paused. "At first, I thought I was doing him a favor by keeping myself separated so that Rasha wouldn't find him. Especially after hearing what she did to Kadir. But now I don't think it was a good idea."

"I haven't spoken to my son either. It has nothing to do with Rasha though."

Baines looked him up and down. "We all know he's not fucking with you because you still on that shit."

Avante looked down in shame. "Yeah, every day of my life."

"So, what do you want, man? Because if it's true she's coming, I want out of town ASAP."

"I found out from somebody that Zeno knows, that she's after our sons and us. Said he couldn't give us a lot of detail but to be careful."

"Zeno cut us off." Baines said. "Why he giving the heads up?"

"I know," Avante said looking around. "I'm as shocked as you are."

"So why you telling me face to face? You never put yourself out for anybody, Avante?"

"I need money to get out of town. If it's true she's back I don't want—"

Suddenly a white van, with Mercy behind the steering wheel, came barreling in their direction. Before they could run for cover, it slammed into both of their legs, pinning them against the fence behind them.

To be sure they were dead, she hopped out of the driver's seat, with The Oxfords behind her for cover. It was obvious they were dead, but she pumped two in each of them anyway.

Nalo's life in prison had been bad. But after speaking to several counselors he understood he had to change, or he would risk making life worse in prison. Especially since he wasn't getting out anytime soon.

When he was first arrested for raping and terrorizing Crystal which resulted in her committing suicide, he was only sentenced to ten years. But the moment he got out, unlike Kadir who tried to live his life right, he participated in sex trafficking and was sentenced to twenty-five years. The way it happened it had set up written all over it, but hindsight is 20/20.

He was in prison on his last day when one of the inmates asked him if he was into making a little money. Since he didn't have any job prospects he immediately said yes. The inmate made a connection and before he knew it, he was meeting young girls in hotels with the intent of using their bodies for his own profit. After only three days in business, the hotel was raided, and he was given life for exploiting young girls.

Back in prison, every day he was fighting somebody. At first, he didn't understand why until someone made it clear. It was Mercy's doing. It was always Mercy's doing.

But now he wanted different. He would try to avoid her traps and make the best of his time.

At least he hoped so.

Nalo was preparing to leave the cafeteria when someone slid him a letter. Since people barely talked to him, he was admittedly suspicious. Opening the letter, it read:

SHE'S COMING.

The words rocked his soul and his eyes widened with fear. Because normally her attacks were of a sneaky nature. But with the heads up it meant he was possibly breathing his last breath.

Living his last days.

At the moment he figured the only thing that could save him was solitary confinement. And so, the first person he saw he stole in the face. As he watched the correctional officers come out of nowhere to get him off the inmate, he realized his plan may work. Even though it could mean a lockdown for six months.

Still, if he was in confinement, at least no one could hurt him.

As the correctional officers hoisted him up off the man and escorted him out of the cafeteria, he didn't make it five feet before two men came up behind him and hit him several times in the back of the head with a hammer.

Although the emergency alarm system was sounded, and the C.O.'s were able to grab them, the damage was already done.

He died in I.C.U.

As Mercy sat in the back of her Aston Martin while being chauffeured to the hospital she thought about a lot of things. Mainly the murder spree she just indulged in which was highly successful.

So why didn't she feel better?

She thought it had always been about getting revenge. She thought it had always been about righting the wrongs.

So where was the relief?

Where was her peace?

To make matters worse, when she was on the way home after killing Avante and Baines, she received a call from the hospital that Sybil may not make it through the night. Stopping everything, she was preparing to go to the hospital when she received one more call.

"We are calling to inform you that Sybil didn't make it. We're sorry."

At first, she felt rage.

"You stupid, bitch! I told you not to make me talk to you!" She said to herself. "I told you not to…"

And then the tears flowed.

This was followed by denial.

Mercy knew she was gone, but she didn't want to accept it. She figured the old woman was just up to her old tricks. And trying to get her to change her life for the better. And at the same time, she knew she would never play with her that way when she knew how much she loved her.

And where was Palmer? Where was her man? Why wasn't he returning her calls? Her life was truly crashing down around her just like Sybil predicted.

"Ma'am, do you want me to take you to the hospital still?" Her driver asked. The car was parked on a side street in what felt like the middle of nowhere.

Using her voice, she said, "Take me to Juno's house."

Fifteen minutes later they were in a seedier part of Baltimore. Juno lived in a brick building that had been renovated but the rest of the neighborhood didn't know it. And as a result, crime was on a high and the streets were always littered with trash.

Knocking on the door once, someone opened it quickly. It was Juno's older sister. Her name was Marikina.

She looked tired.

She looked hurt.

And she looked fed up.

Just like Mercy.

"I didn't know you were coming." She crossed her arms over her chest. "I don't know if you heard, but Juno lost the baby."

She did know. She set the entire thing up. "Can I come in?"

The moment Marikina heard her voice shivers shot up her spine. Just like the rest of the world knew, she didn't speak to you directly unless your life meant nothing.

Was she a dead woman walking?

"Oh, um, sure you can." She opened the door wider. "But are we cool?"

"I just wanna see Juno."

Walking back to Juno's room she opened her bedroom door without an invite and saw her sitting up in bed, looking out of the window. Her hair was all over her head. Her eyes were red, and she looked ripped down. It was exactly how a woman would look who just lost their child.

Although she didn't have any ill will towards her, Juno could still be considered one of her victims based on what she did to her life.

"How do you feel?" Mercy asked.

Juno spoke softly, while looking down. "I can't believe I let you kill my baby. What...what is wrong with me?"

Mercy had planned to be a little softer with her at first. After all, she did lose a child. But after being blamed off the top, she tapped into that place of resentment that she always held near. "Listen, bitch, I paid you $100,000. And you accepted it. So, you killed your own fucking baby!"

Juno shook her head softly and wiped the tears that creeped up on her face with two fists. "You're right. You're fucking right and this will haunt me forever." She took a long breath and said, "But what did Zeno do to make you hate him so much? What did my family do besides love you that made you hate us so much?"

Mercy looked down. For the first time ever, she felt a little guilt. Was it because Sybil had died? And that she didn't know where Palmer was?

"Bezeno betrayed me. And I know he wanted a son. He always talked about having a son. But just so you know, the baby situation wasn't supposed to be you. Originally it was going to be his first baby's mother. But she birthed a daughter instead. And I needed it to be a boy."

"How did he break your heart?" She shook her head. "I killed my baby for you. I need to know what it was all about."

Mercy knew nothing she said would justify the loss. "He slept with my friend." She sighed. "And that's all you need to know. Now, have you seen your cousin? I have been looking for him all night."

Suddenly a flood of tears escaped Juno's eyes and she cried hard. Pointing behind herself she said, "They left him in there. For you."

Mercy felt gut-punched.

All the time she spent talking to her ass, she could have been holding Palmer in her arms.

Quickly she ran to the bedroom she said he was located and pushed the door open. And there his body was, lying on the bed with his throat slit. His beautiful skin had greyed out, leaving what already had begun to look like a corpse.

Kicking her shoes off, she ran to his bedside and dropped to her knees.

Now she was finally realizing what it felt like to lose someone you truly loved. To lose someone who truly loved you back.

"I told you," she said to him shaking her head. "I told you this would happen." She wept long and hard.

Enraged, she removed her boxcutter and ripped at his face with the tip. She hated him for making her love him. And more than anything, she hated that he was gone.

She was still cutting at his face, when she heard Marikina talking to someone outside. "She's in the room like you asked." She said with disdain. "Now get that bitch out of my sister's house."

The moment she heard her voice, her eyebrows rose as she realized she walked into a trap. Now that she thought about it, the set up made sense. Of course, they would come to Juno's house. Of course, they would know where she lived. After all, Bezeno was Juno's baby's mother. And had she not lost Sybil and Palmer in one night, she would have thought clearer.

It didn't matter now.

It was eventide.

As she ran.

Fast.

While she made her escape, tiny shards of glass stabbed into the heels of her feet as she took off in the dark alley. In fear for her life, her stomach twirled as she looked behind her for who she knew was coming.

Unfortunately, she didn't make it far.

Because Bezeno's men covered both ends of the alley.

When she tripped and fell, within a matter of seconds, he was upon her. Towering over her frame he said, "Did I deserve this level of pain?" He yelled.

Silence.

"Fucking answer me, bitch!"

"Please don't hurt me." She begged.

"All I did was try to love you. All I did was try to protect you. But you could never see me. And the moment I make a mistake by fucking a girl I didn't know you knew, you set out to ruin my life."

"I didn't do −."

"You poisoned my son while in the womb, knowing how bad it would hurt me." He lowered his voice. "Are you…are you even sorry?"

This was the time for things to change.

This was the turning point that could have made the difference in her life. All she had to do was admit her wrong. All she had to do was let the rage go.

And maybe things would be forgiven.

Instead she raised her head high and said, "You shouldn't have fucked that bitch! Fuck you and that baby."

Lowering his height, he wrapped his hands around her throat and squeezed the life out of her body. It was slight at first and then he squeezed more.

BY T. STYLES

It was surprising…

She was easy to kill.

Based on how much pain she caused, he thought it would be harder.

He was wrong.

Darcy was the only person who showed up to Mercy's funeral.

It was easy to understand why. So many people hated her that it was a wonder that she lived as long as she did.

And still, despite it all she was still her baby sister.

As far as Darcy was concerned her sister's life would not be in vain. She would live each moment focusing on the best of life. She would only think about the good in other people.

And she would live each day as if it really mattered.

Because it did.

With her work done, Darcy took a deep breath. Because she knew her sister was now at peace.

COMING SOON

TRUCE

TWO

THE WAR OF THE LOU'S

T. STYLES

BY T. STYLES

CARTEL PUBLICATIONS

PRESENTS

The Cartel Publications Order Form

www.thecartelpublications.com

Inmates **ONLY** receive novels for $10.00 per book **PLUS** shipping fee **PER BOOK.**

(Mail Order **MUST** come from inmate directly to receive discount)

Shyt List 1	_____	$15.00
Shyt List 2	_____	$15.00
Shyt List 3	_____	$15.00
Shyt List 4	_____	$15.00
Shyt List 5	_____	$15.00
Shyt List 6	_____	$15.00
Pitbulls In A Skirt	_____	$15.00
Pitbulls In A Skirt 2	_____	$15.00
Pitbulls In A Skirt 3	_____	$15.00
Pitbulls In A Skirt 4	_____	$15.00
Pitbulls In A Skirt 5	_____	$15.00
Victoria's Secret	_____	$15.00
Poison 1	_____	$15.00
Poison 2	_____	$15.00
Hell Razor Honeys	_____	$15.00
Hell Razor Honeys 2	_____	$15.00
A Hustler's Son	_____	$15.00
A Hustler's Son 2	_____	$15.00
Black and Ugly	_____	$15.00
Black and Ugly As Ever	_____	$15.00
Ms Wayne & The Queens of DC **(LGBT)**	_____	$15.00
Black And The Ugliest	_____	$15.00
Year Of The Crackmom	_____	$15.00
Deadheads	_____	$15.00
The Face That Launched A Thousand Bullets	_____	$15.00
The Unusual Suspects	_____	$15.00
Paid In Blood	_____	$15.00
Raunchy	_____	$15.00
Raunchy 2	_____	$15.00
Raunchy 3	_____	$15.00
Mad Maxxx (4th Book Raunchy Series)	_____	$15.00
Quita's Dayscare Center	_____	$15.00
Quita's Dayscare Center 2	_____	$15.00
Pretty Kings	_____	$15.00
Pretty Kings 2	_____	$15.00
Pretty Kings 3	_____	$15.00
Pretty Kings 4	_____	$15.00
Silence Of The Nine	_____	$15.00
Silence Of The Nine 2	_____	$15.00
Silence Of The Nine 3	_____	$15.00

ASK THE STREETS FOR MERCY   309

Prison Throne _____	$15.00
Drunk & Hot Girls _____	$15.00
Hersband Material (LGBT) _____	$15.00
The End: How To Write A _____	$15.00
Bestselling Novel In 30 Days (Non-Fiction Guide)	
Upscale Kittens _____	$15.00
Wake & Bake Boys _____	$15.00
Young & Dumb _____	$15.00
Young & Dumb 2: Vyce's Getback _____	$15.00
Tranny 911 (LGBT) _____	$15.00
Tranny 911: Dixie's Rise (LGBT) _____	$15.00
First Comes Love, Then Comes Murder _____	$15.00
Luxury Tax	$15.00
The Lying King _____	$15.00
Crazy Kind Of Love _____	$15.00
Goon _____	$15.00
And They Call Me God _____	$15.00
The Ungrateful Bastards _____	$15.00
Lipstick Dom (LGBT) _____	$15.00
A School of Dolls (LGBT) _____	$15.00
Hoetic Justice _____	$15.00
KALI: Raunchy Relived _____	$15.00
(5th Book in Raunchy Series)	
Skeezers _____	$15.00
Skeezers 2 _____	$15.00
You Kissed Me, Now I Own You _____	$15.00
Nefarious _____	$15.00
Redbone 3: The Rise of The Fold _____	$15.00
The Fold (4th Redbone Book) _____	$15.00
Clown Niggas _____	$15.00
The One You Shouldn't Trust _____	$15.00
The WHORE The Wind	
Blew My Way _____	$15.00
She Brings The Worst Kind _____	$15.00
The House That Crack Built _____	$15.00
The House That Crack Built 2 _____	$15.00
The House That Crack Built 3 _____	$15.00
The House That Crack Built 4 _____	$15.00
Level Up (LGBT) _____	$15.00
Villains: It's Savage Season _____	$15.00
Gay For My Bae _____	$15.00
War _____	$15.00
War 2: All Hell Breaks Loose _____	$15.00
War 3: The Land Of The Lou's _____	$15.00
War 4: Skull Island _____	$15.00
War 5: Karma _____	$15.00
War 6: Envy _____	$15.00
War 7: Pink Cotton _____	$15.00
Madjesty vs. Jayden (Novella) _____	$8.99
You Left Me No Choice _____	$15.00
Truce – A War Saga _____	$15.00
Ask The Streets For Mercy _____	$15.00
Truce 2 - The War of The Lou's _____	$15.00

(**Redbone 1 & 2** are **NOT** Cartel Publications novels and if **ordered** the cost is **FULL** price of $15.00 **each**. **No Exceptions**.)

Please add **$5.00** for shipping and handling fees for up to **(2) BOOKS PER ORDER**. (INMATES INCLUDED) (See next page for details)

The Cartel Publications * P.O. BOX 486 OWINGS MILLS MD 21117

Name: _____

Address: _____

City/State: _____

Contact/Email: _____

Please allow 10-15 BUSINESS days Before shipping.

***PLEASE NOTE DUE TO __COVID-19__ SOME ORDERS MAY TAKE UP TO __3 WEEKS OR
LONGER__
BEFORE THEY SHIP***

The Cartel Publications is __NOT__ responsible for __Prison Orders__ rejected!

__NO RETURNS and NO REFUNDS__
__NO PERSONAL CHECKS ACCEPTED__
__STAMPS NO LONGER ACCEPTED__

CPSIA information can be obtained
at www.ICGtesting.com
Printed in the USA
LVHW041743150920
666084LV00002B/232

9 781948 373289